# *The Case of the Dangerous Solution*

As she reached Crouse's office doorway, Nancy noticed a small, darkened room next to it. A sign on the door said Absolutely No Entry. Property of Jerald Crouse. Violators Will Be Subject to Severe Penalties.

Nancy felt a flutter in her heart. Was Crouse working on some kind of secret project? Darting a glance over her shoulder, Nancy stepped inside the off-limits room.

The tiny lab had counters on three sides. On them sat papers, beakers, test tubes, charts, and unmarked glass bottles. Nancy took a step toward the counter to the right and tried to make out what was written on a pad.

Suddenly a voice came from behind her. "Get out of there now, Ms. Drew!"

With a gasp, Nancy spun around. . . .

# Nancy Drew Mystery Stories

#57 The Triple Hoax
#58 The Flying Saucer Mystery
#62 The Kachina Doll Mystery
#63 The Twin Dilemma
#67 The Sinister Omen
#68 The Elusive Heiress
#70 The Broken Anchor
#72 The Haunted Carousel
#73 Enemy Match
#76 The Eskimo's Secret
#77 The Bluebeard Room
#78 The Phantom of Venice
#79 The Double Horror of Fenley Place
#81 The Mardi Gras Mystery
#87 The Case of the Rising Stars
#89 The Case of the Disappearing Deejay
#91 The Girl Who Couldn't Remember
#92 The Ghost of Craven Cove
#93 The Case of the Safecracker's Secret
#94 The Picture-Perfect Mystery
#97 The Mystery at Magnolia Mansion
#98 The Haunting of Horse Island
#99 The Secret of Seven Rocks
#101 The Mystery of the Missing Millionairess
#102 The Secret in the Dark
#103 The Stranger in the Shadows
#104 The Mystery of the Jade Tiger
#105 The Clue in the Antique Trunk
#106 The Case of the Artful Crime
#108 The Secret of the Tibetan Treasure
#109 The Mystery of the Masked Rider
#110 The Nutcracker Ballet Mystery
#111 The Secret at Solaire
#112 Crime in the Queen's Court
#113 The Secret Lost at Sea
#114 The Search for the Silver Persian
#115 The Suspect in the Smoke
#116 The Case of the Twin Teddy Bears
#117 Mystery on the Menu
#118 Trouble at Lake Tahoe
#119 The Mystery of the Missing Mascot
#120 The Case of the Floating Crime
#121 The Fortune-Teller's Secret
#122 The Message in the Haunted Mansion
#123 The Clue on the Silver Screen
#124 The Secret of the Scarlet Hand
#125 The Teen Model Mystery
#126 The Riddle in the Rare Book
#127 The Case of the Dangerous Solution
#128 The Treasure in the Royal Tower
#129 The Baby-sitter Burglaries
#130 The Sign of the Falcon
#131 The Hidden Inheritance
#132 The Fox Hunt Mystery
#133 The Mystery at the Crystal Palace
#134 The Secret of the Forgotten Cave
#135 The Riddle of the Ruby Gazelle
#136 The Wedding Day Mystery
#137 In Search of the Black Rose
#138 The Legend of the Lost Gold
#139 The Secret of Candlelight Inn
#140 The Door-to-Door Deception
#141 The Wild Cat Crime

## Available from MINSTREL Books

For orders other than by individual consumers, Pocket Books grants a discount on the purchase of **10 or more** copies of single titles for special markets or premium use. For further details, please write to the Vice-President of Special Markets, Pocket Books, 1633 Broadway, New York, NY 10019-6785, 8th Floor.

For information on how individual consumers can place orders, please write to Mail Order Department, Simon & Schuster Inc., 200 Old Tappan Road, Old Tappan, NJ 07675.

NANCY DREW MYSTERY STORIES®

127

# NANCY DREW®

# THE CASE OF THE DANGEROUS SOLUTION

CAROLYN KEENE

Published by POCKET BOOKS
New York London Toronto Sydney Tokyo Singapore

This book is a work of fiction. Names, characters, places and incidents are products of the author's imagination or are used fictitiously. Any resemblance to actual events or locales or persons, living or dead, is entirely coincidental.

A MINSTREL PAPERBACK *Original*

A Minstrel Book published by
POCKET BOOKS, a division of Simon & Schuster Inc.
1230 Avenue of the Americas, New York, NY 10020



Produced by Mega-Books, Inc.



ISBN: 0-671-50500-9

First Minstrel Books printing October 1995

10 9 8 7 6 5 4



Cover art by Aleta Jenks

Printed in the U.S.A.

# Contents

# 1

## *Danger on Delivery*

"I've got it!" Bess Marvin said, swinging her blond ponytail as she turned toward Nancy Drew and Regina Houser. Continuing down the sidewalk with her friends, Bess asked, "What if I write my essay about my summer as a camp counselor?"

Nancy and Regina glanced at each other and smiled. Regina had been in Nancy and Bess's class at River Heights High School. Trying not to laugh, Nancy said, "You mean when you sank the camp's sailboat and got lost in the woods with a group of campers?" Her blue eyes crinkled in amusement. "Do you want your whole creative writing class to know about that?"

Bess winced. "Uh, maybe not."

Regina smiled. "My brother, DeWitt, would never let you live that down," she said. DeWitt was in Bess's summer creative writing class at River Heights Community College.

"Maybe George will have some ideas," Nancy suggested. The three girls, having just finished breakfast at a local coffee shop, were on their way to visit Bess's cousin, George Fayne. George had a part-time summer job delivering prescriptions for Twickham's Drugstore, which was only a couple blocks away. Twickham's had been in downtown River Heights for as long as Nancy could remember.

Though she had known Bess and George almost her whole life, Nancy could never get over how different they were. Tall, dark George loved the outdoors and almost every sport. Blond-haired Bess was much more comfortable curled up in front of a fireplace with a good romance novel.

A few moments later Nancy, Bess, and Regina arrived at a small brick building with an orange neon sign that said Twickham's in curving script. As Nancy pushed the door open, a little brass bell tinkled. The three girls paused inside the door and looked around.

Nancy's father, Carson Drew, always said that Twickham's looked just as it did when he was a boy. Though the store carried many modern conveniences, from blank videotapes to contact lens solution, it still had the smell of a different era: a sweet blend of talcum powder, penny candy, and medicinal tonics. The aisles were narrow, but the ceiling was high, with wooden paddle fans cooling the air. There was even an old-fashioned soda fountain, located to Nancy's right, against the front window.

On a side wall, behind a polished wooden counter, was the pharmacy area, raised a step from the rest of the drugstore. The pharmacy's narrow shelves were full of small bottles of pills, syrups, and other medicines—it was the best-stocked pharmacy in town, Nancy remembered her dad saying. In front of it, the cashier's counter had a heavy brass cash register that looked like an antique.

Nancy remembered the store's owner, Martin Twickham, whose smiling face used to greet customers at the pharmacy counter. She knew he had retired a few years ago, though he still owned the store. She missed seeing him.

"Hey, are you ladies going to buy anything, or are you just blocking the doorway?"

Nancy turned around to see George entering the drugstore with a big grin on her face. Carrying a small, blue zippered bag for her delivery money, George as usual didn't stop moving. "Come on up to the pharmacy and say hi," she greeted her friends.

Nancy, Bess, and Regina followed George up into the pharmacy area, past the short line of customers waiting for their prescriptions. The pharmacy was a long narrow room, with floor-to-ceiling shelves on one side. Behind the counter, a man and woman in white lab coats stood before computer screens.

"Hi, Grace," George called out, waving to the woman in the white lab coat. She was about forty, with chin-length, very curly black hair. Nancy knew she was Grace Cerrito, the head pharmacist and George's boss.

But Grace seemed not to have heard George. She had just turned, scowling, to the man at her right. "I can't waste time every morning double-checking your counts from the night before," she snapped at him.

The man's face reddened. "You don't have to," he mumbled, keeping his eyes glued to the computer screen. "I only got it wrong once."

"That's one time too many," Grace said in a low, tight voice. Then, with a quick sigh, she looked up at the girls. A big smile lit up her face. "What brings you guys here so early in the morning?" she asked. Her voice was totally cheerful again.

Nancy could tell that her friends were embarrassed about overhearing the exchange between Grace and the other pharmacist. She herself was very curious about it. But she broke the awkward silence, saying, "Oh, uh, we're checking up on George, making sure she's doing her work."

Grace laughed, her eyes crinkling merrily. "You don't have to do that, Nancy," she said.

"George is doing fine. We're very grateful for her help." Nancy smiled in reply.

Bess, who already knew Grace, said hello, and George introduced Grace to Regina. "And this is Kevin Duffy," George added, gesturing toward the other pharmacist.

Kevin Duffy's eyes were still glued to his computer screen. At George's words he looked over, running his hand nervously through his longish, curly, light brown hair. The expression on his tanned face was sullen, as though he was still smarting from Grace's rebuke. As George introduced Nancy, Bess, and Regina, Kevin simply nodded, barely even looking their way. Clearly, they had caught him at a bad time.

"Hey, Kevin," George said, trying to lighten things up. "I saw your favorite team squeaked by in that doubleheader yesterday."

"Nah," he said. "They had it in the bag the whole time."

"Oh, right!" George said with a laugh. She turned to the others. "Kevin's a big Steamers fan," she explained, referring to a local minor-league baseball team. "And the way they've been playing, that's not easy," she added with a teasing smile.

Her remark coaxed a little grin onto Kevin's face, though he never stopped tapping on his keyboard. He swiveled in his chair to begin counting pills on a small tray and putting them in a plastic bottle.

George turned away to let him concentrate on his work. "So what have you three been up to?" she asked her friends.

Regina laughed. "Food—what else? We just came from breakfast." She glanced at her watch. "But I'm afraid I've got to get going. I have to be at work in fifteen minutes."

"Oh!" Bess said. "That must mean it's almost time for my class." She looked at her friends in a panic. "And I still don't have a topic for my essay!"

"I'll give you a lift—I drive by the college anyway," Regina offered. "We can brainstorm ideas on the way."

After Regina and Bess said goodbye and left, Grace called George over to her work area and said, "George, that face cream we special-ordered for Mrs. Cay came in last night. She didn't ask for it to be delivered, but if you have time, maybe you could drop it by her house."

"Sure thing," George said. "I always like to see Mrs. Cay."

Grace smiled warmly. "She's great, isn't she?" she agreed. "Say hello to her for me."

Nancy began to back away. "I should let you get to work," she said to George.

"Hang on," George said. "If you're not doing anything, why don't you come with me on this delivery run? It'll just take a few minutes." She turned to Grace. "Is that okay, Grace?"

"No problem," Grace said. "Just hurry back. We're having a busy morning."

George slipped the jar of face cream into a paper bag and wrote out a delivery receipt. Then she led Nancy out the back entrance to the asphalt parking lot behind the drugstore. They got into a small blue car with the word *Twickham's* painted on the doors, along with the store's phone number.

Nancy watched the morning traffic as George steered the car out onto the busy downtown street that ran beside the drugstore. "You seem to be enjoying this job," she commented.

George nodded enthusiastically. "It's turning out to be a cool place to work," she said. "Doing deliveries means I can get out and move around a lot. Most of the customers have been coming to Twickham's for years, so they know all the employees. Delivering to them is more like doing a favor for a friend than doing a job."

"Except that you get paid for it," Nancy added.

George smiled. "Yeah, that is nice," she admitted. "This is the last place in town that offers free delivery service, and the customers really appreciate it. Most of them tip me nicely. I'm saving for a new CD player."

George drove into an older section of River Heights. "This is one of my favorite parts of town," Nancy said, looking at the small, neat houses lining the residential blocks. "Even though these homes have been around awhile, people really keep them looking nice. Each house here seems to have its own personality."

"Mrs. Cay told me that she's lived here her whole life," George said. "And she's been a customer at Twickham's since it opened, over forty years ago. She's about seventy, I think, though she's still sharp as a tack."

Nancy smiled. "Sounds like she's one of your favorite customers."

George grinned and nodded as she turned onto a shady side street. "I hope I'm like her when I get to be that age," she said. "It seems like she's always got some new project going—she's always trying to help out someone else. And she still rides her bike around town."

George pulled the car up to a one-story brick house covered with ivy. The small lawn was bordered with neatly trimmed bushes, and bright flowers lined the walk. More flowers filled rows of pots on the porch. "Someone here has a green thumb," Nancy commented as she and George stepped out of the delivery car.

"That's Mrs. Cay all right," George said as they headed up the stone walkway. "She can grow just about any—"

George broke off suddenly, staring at the front of the house. Nancy came to a halt as she noticed the same thing George had.

"Why is her front door standing wide open?" George asked in a low voice.

"Maybe she stepped outside for a moment," Nancy said. Her eyes swept over the porch and the sides of the house, hoping to spot Mrs. Cay.

Nancy and George made their way onto the porch. George hesitated, then raised her hand to knock on the half-open door.

Suddenly, from inside Mrs. Cay's house, they heard a man's voice cry out, "Oh, no!"

# 2

## *A Medical Mystery*

Nancy ran through Mrs. Cay's open door, with George at her heels. "Hello?" Nancy called out as she dashed across a small living room.

"In here!" a man replied.

Nancy followed the voice to the back of the house. As she charged into a sunny kitchen, she pulled up short.

An elderly woman lay sprawled across the linoleum floor. Her arms and legs were twitching, as if she were having some kind of convulsion.

"Mrs. Cay!" George cried out from behind Nancy.

A tall man in his forties was kneeling beside the woman, trying to hold down her shoulders. He glanced up at Nancy and George, his eyes wide with panic. "Aunt Evelyn!" he yelled. "What's wrong with her?"

A horrible gasping sound came from the woman. Her eyelids fluttered, and her neck snapped into a rigid, fixed position.

"What happened?" Nancy asked the man kneeling by Mrs. Cay.

"I—I don't know," he stammered. "She just collapsed onto the floor a moment ago. I called an ambulance right away—" He broke off, overcome with anxiety.

Nancy and George knelt beside him on the floor. George tried to hold Mrs. Cay's head steady. "Can she breathe?" George asked.

"I don't know," he said hoarsely. "She doesn't answer me."

Feeling helpless, Nancy watched the poor woman straining for breath. What was wrong with Mrs. Cay? Nancy reached out to hold one of the woman's stiff arms, but as she touched her, suddenly the twitching stopped and Mrs. Cay went limp. "She's lost consciousness," Nancy said grimly.

"Where is that ambulance?" George asked in a tense voice.

"Oh, no!" the man groaned. "What—" Then he broke off. In the distance, they heard the sound of a wailing siren.

"Thank goodness," George said.

Nancy jumped up and ran to the door to meet the paramedics. The ambulance squealed to a stop in front of the brick house, and two emergency technicians, a man and a woman, jumped from the cab. Nancy hurriedly led them back to the kitchen. George and the tall man moved out of the way as the technicians kneeled down on either side of the unconscious woman. "What happened?" said the female technician.

"I don't know," the tall man said. "I just stopped by a few minutes ago, and Aunt Evelyn was sitting here with a cup of tea. I'm her nephew, Don Cay. We were talking when suddenly she began gasping and having some kind of spasm. She fell out of her chair, totally losing control. That's when these two young women arrived," he added, nodding toward Nancy and George.

"We were making a drugstore delivery," George explained. "When we got here Mrs. Cay was having some sort of seizure, and then she went unconscious."

As Don Cay and George spoke, the technicians were prying open Mrs. Cay's eyes and taking her pulse. The male technician placed a portable oxygen mask over her mouth. "We'll put her on a respirator in the truck and get her right to the emergency room," he said.

"But what's wrong with her?" Don Cay asked, his face twisted with worry.

The technician shook his head. "I don't know," he said simply. "Is she in good health?"

Both George and Don Cay nodded. "She has a cold, but other than that, she's fine," Don said.

"She's never had a serious health problem in her entire life."

"Let's get the gurney," the female technician said. In a matter of seconds, the paramedics had strapped Mrs. Cay to a gurney and carried her to the ambulance. Don Cay climbed in the back with her, and Nancy and George followed the ambulance to River Heights General Hospital.

"Oh, Nancy, what do you think has happened to Mrs. Cay?" George said as she weaved the delivery car through traffic, trying to keep up with the ambulance.

Nancy bit her lip. "I don't know," she said.

"Could it be a stroke or a heart attack?" George asked in an uneasy voice.

"It didn't look like a heart attack," Nancy reassured George. "She wasn't clutching at her chest. But we'll have to see what the doctor says."

George found a parking spot on a side street, and the two girls made their way to the admitting desk of the hospital's emergency room. Looking in the waiting room, Nancy saw Don Cay just hanging up a pay phone.

Nancy and George walked over to him. Nancy hesitated to intrude on him, but he looked so grateful when he saw the girls, she realized they might be some comfort to him at this stressful time. Besides, Don Cay was the only person who had witnessed Mrs. Cay's mysterious collapse—

and Nancy couldn't help wondering what had happened.

"Hello," he said in a tone of relief. "It was nice of you to come. The doctor's examining Aunt Ev now." The tall man's blue eyes were wide with worry, and he looked tired. "My wife should be here soon," he added.

"I know you must've spoken to the doctor already," Nancy began gently, "but I wondered if you noticed anything strange about your aunt this morning."

Don Cay shook his head in despair. "As I just said to my wife, Aunt Ev looked perfectly fine," he replied. "That cold she'd had really bothered her, but this morning when I called she said her head was clearing up. I had an extra symphony ticket for tomorrow evening, so I stopped by on my way to work this morning to give it to her. She seemed to be her usual energetic self and was just finishing a midmorning cup of tea. She was sitting at the table when she started convulsing, and . . . fell, and . . . well, you saw the rest," Don said, trailing off.

Nancy nodded sympathetically. It was frustrating to have no clue as to why Mrs. Cay collapsed, but Don Cay had only been with her for a couple of minutes. Maybe he would remember something after he had calmed down.

Suddenly Don Cay looked up sharply. "Oh, Dr. Volman, what is it?" he said.

Nancy turned to see a middle-aged man with

graying hair and mustache walking toward them. His clothes were rumpled, as if he had spent the night in them at the hospital. He wore a concerned look on his dark face as he tucked a pen into his front breast pocket. "Your aunt is on a respirator and is stabilized now," he said to Don Cay. "But she's still comatose."

"But what happened to her?" Don Cay asked impatiently.

The doctor shook his head. "It's too early for me to say," he said. "It's not a heart attack, as you were wondering. But we'll have to run several tests and get the lab results back before I'll be able to determine what's happened. By any chance do you know what your aunt had for breakfast or for dinner last night?"

Mrs. Cay's nephew looked surprised. "No, I don't," he said. "She's generally a light eater, and she's had a cold, so I doubt she's been eating very much."

"Do you think this is a reaction to something she ate?" Nancy asked Dr. Volman.

"I'm not prepared to make a definitive diagnosis," the doctor said cautiously, "but a sudden, violent reaction like Mrs. Cay's could come from something she ingested."

"We'll try to find out what she's eaten," Don Cay offered.

"Good," the doctor said. "I've called her doctor for her complete medical history, but I haven't heard back from him yet. Perhaps you can help with that—see if you can find any medical records at home. Between that and the lab tests, we should be able to reach a diagnosis."

Don Cay nodded wearily. "Can I see her now?" he asked before Dr. Volman left.

Dr. Volman frowned. "I'd really like to have time to do some blood work and move her into a room. After that, you can certainly visit her." The doctor nodded goodbye and walked swiftly back to the patient area.

George put out her hand to Don Cay and said, "Please let me know if you hear anything. You can reach me at Twickham's—my name is George Fayne." Don Cay shook her hand and gave her a thankful smile.

Nancy reached out to shake his hand as well. "And I'm Nancy Drew," she said. Then she hesitated. "Will you be heading back to your aunt's house now?" she asked gently.

Don Cay sighed. "I guess so," he said. "I need to pick up my car, anyway."

"Would you mind if I went with you?" Nancy asked. "Maybe I can find something that could help us figure out what happened to her."

"Nancy has quite a reputation as a detective here in River Heights," George put in. "There's never been a mystery she couldn't solve."

Don Cay blinked, looking bewildered. "In that case, I'd appreciate your help," he admitted. "I'd really like to know what happened to Aunt Evelyn. This whole thing just seems so strange."

A few moments later, Don Cay's wife, Rosemary, arrived. She agreed to stay with Mrs. Cay in case her condition changed. "Someone should be with her when she wakes up," Rosemary said. George offered to drive Don Cay and Nancy back to Mrs. Cay's house on her way back to work at Twickham's.

As George dropped them off in front of Mrs. Cay's small brick house, Nancy thought to herself that the house already seemed forlorn. Mrs. Cay's red bike stood on the corner of the porch, locked to the rail. And though the potted flowers still waved cheerfully with the slight breeze, there was an emptiness about the place. As she and Don Cay made their way up the walk, Nancy hoped that Mrs. Cay would be able to return home soon.

After climbing the steps to the front porch, Don Cay opened the door and stepped in. Nancy began to follow him into the silent house.

Suddenly a loud, hoarse shout cut through the quiet neighborhood behind her. "Hey! What do you think you're doing?"

Nancy whirled around. Her eyes widened in surprise.

On the opposite side of the street, his arms folded across his chest and a scowl on his face, stood the assistant pharmacist from Twickham's—Kevin Duffy.

# 3

## *Searching for . . . What?*

What was Kevin Duffy doing here? Nancy wondered uneasily. She stepped down from Mrs. Cay's porch and walked toward the pharmacist, who was glaring at Nancy with narrowed green eyes. Don Cay had already gone on inside his aunt's house.

"I said, what are you doing here?" Duffy called out again sharply as he strode across the street.

"Mrs. Cay is in the hospital," Nancy answered, watching his face carefully for a reaction.

The scowl faded from Duffy's face. "What?" he said in confusion.

Nancy briefly told him what had happened. As she described Mrs. Cay's collapse, Duffy glanced away. "Is she okay now?" he asked in a tight voice.

"The convulsions have stopped, but she's still

unconscious," Nancy reported. "But what are you doing here?"

Kevin Duffy seemed to squirm slightly, and he dug his hands into the pockets of his khaki pants. "Oh, I . . . I was just worried about Mrs. Cay," he mumbled. "I knew she had a cold. I, uh, figured I'd use my break time to check up on her." Beneath his tan, his cheeks flushed as he shifted his weight nervously from foot to foot. Then, abruptly, Kevin turned around and began walking back across the street. "I've got to get back to work," he called gruffly over his shoulder.

Nancy watched as the assistant pharmacist stepped quickly to his small black truck, got in, and started the engine. Jerking it into gear, he sped down the street without a glance back at Nancy.

Kevin Duffy was sure acting strange just now, Nancy thought as she turned back toward the house. Why had he snapped at her when he first saw her? Why had he been so nervous when she asked why he was there? He had to be hiding something. But what?

Nancy pushed open the front door again, almost bumping into Don Cay. "I wondered where you went," he said to her.

Nancy forced a smile. She didn't want to tell Mrs. Cay's nephew about her run-in with Kevin Duffy. The poor man had enough to worry about.

Instead, she said, "Sorry. I was admiring the flowers out front."

Don Cay nodded and his tense face relaxed into a little smile. "Aunt Ev has quite a green thumb," he said. "You should see her vegetable garden out back. She grows some of the best tomatoes in town."

Nancy followed him into the cozy living room she and George had dashed through only an hour earlier. Around a thick, round braided rug were grouped a plump sofa and a rocking chair with a needlepoint basket beside it. Knickknacks were carefully displayed on shelves, and not an item looked to be out of place.

As they entered the kitchen, Nancy could see Don Cay tense a little as he looked around the sunlit, pale yellow room. Nancy herself could still picture Mrs. Cay lying unconscious on the white linoleum floor. She drew a deep breath.

Don Cay pointed to the teacup and saucer on the table and the small plate in the sink. "I guess that's what she had for her breakfast," he said. "Tea and toast, as always." Nancy peered into the sink to see crumbs of toast still left on the plate.

"I'm going to get her records file from her bedroom closet and see if I can find any medical information," Don Cay said. "Feel free to poke around if you think it'll help." Nancy watched him walk through the dining room into the bedroom, knowing how worried he must feel.

She turned back to the kitchen table and lifted

Mrs. Cay's now-cold cup of tea. She sniffed it carefully but could smell nothing but tea leaves. Then she opened the refrigerator. Several kinds of jams and jellies lined the door, but the main shelves were almost empty. Small cartons of milk and orange juice, a dish of butter, a couple of apples, a cooked chicken breast, and a box of baking soda were the only items there. Nancy noted that the milk and orange juice were fresh.

Nancy then opened all of Mrs. Cay's cupboards, where she found dishes, canned foods, a half-used loaf of bread, pots and pans, cleaning supplies, and the usual baking goods: flour, sugar, baking powder, spices, oils, and nuts. She checked inside each open container, but nothing seemed spoiled.

Next Nancy peered into the garbage bin under the sink and found some used paper towels, an empty orange-juice carton, and some wet tea leaves—nothing out of the ordinary.

She passed through the dining room and reached the door of Mrs. Cay's cheery bedroom. Don Cay was sitting on his aunt's bed, riffling through some papers next to a gray metal file box. He looked up. "Find anything?" he asked. Nancy shook her head.

"These are her medical records," he said. He nodded toward the small hallway. "There's a guest room and the bathroom down there, if you want to check those out."

"Thanks," Nancy said. She went straight to the

bathroom, opening the medicine cabinet above the large, old-fashioned sink. There she found the usual assortment of personal items: toothpaste, bandages, nail files, soap, cotton balls. The top shelf held aspirin, antiseptic ointment, and some prescription bottles from Twickham's—antibiotics and ointments. Nancy closed the medicine cabinet and gazed around the spotless bathroom. As in every other room in the house, nothing seemed out of place or unusual here.

Nancy walked back to Mrs. Cay's bedroom, feeling more puzzled than ever. She could find no clue as to the elderly woman's collapse. Of course, Nancy reminded herself, anything could be a clue, since she didn't know what she was looking for.

Don Cay was just putting his aunt's file box back in her closet as Nancy returned to the bedroom. "Well?" he said. "Any theories?"

Nancy sighed. "I'd like to say yes," she said. "But nothing here seems out of order."

He nodded. "I'm confused, too," he said. "I can't imagine what caused that fit of hers." He glanced at his watch. "I'd better get back to the hospital and give these records to Dr. Volman," he said. "Do you want a ride somewhere?"

"How about dropping me off at Twickham's?" Nancy asked. "My car's parked by the drugstore."

"Sure," he said. The two of them walked back

out through the quiet living room. Nancy was still glancing about, hoping for a last-minute clue.

She paused on the front porch as Don Cay locked his aunt's front door. Her eyes glided over the empty flowerpots, little spades, weed killer, and watering can lined up on the porch. She hoped Mrs. Cay would be able to return to her gardening soon.

Within a few minutes Don Cay had dropped off Nancy in front of Twickham's. She walked beneath the tinkling bell into the drugstore again. The store was busier than it had been earlier, but as Nancy reached the pharmacy, there was only one customer waiting. George was behind the counter, her head bent as she counted out money from her delivery bag. Grace Cerrito and Kevin Duffy were working at their computers.

"Oh, Nancy, hello!" Grace called out to her. Both George and Kevin Duffy looked up. Nancy noticed Duffy's eyes narrowing as he caught sight of her.

Grace leaned over the counter toward Nancy. "George told me about Evelyn Cay," she said in a low, urgent voice. "I can't imagine what's happened to that poor woman."

"Did you find anything at her house?" George asked Nancy.

Nancy shook her head glumly. "Nothing. I did a pretty thorough search after you left," she said to Kevin Duffy pointedly. At her words, the assistant pharmacist's shoulders tensed up.

Grace spun around to look at him. "After *you* left?" she said. "What were you doing there?"

Duffy flushed and dropped the bottle of pills he was filling. "I don't know what she's talking about," he said crossly, trying to sweep up the spilled pills from the counter. "She must have mistaken me for someone else."

Nancy looked at Kevin Duffy curiously. She had deliberately mentioned his being at Mrs. Cay's house to test his reaction. He had responded with a lie. Why? Nancy wondered.

Grace turned back to Nancy. "Did you really see Kevin, dear?" she asked.

Nancy stole one more glance at Kevin Duffy, then looked at Grace, shaking her head in apparent confusion. "I thought so," she said. "But with everything that was going on, maybe I was wrong." She could see relief flood his flushed face. She told herself she'd have to ask him about it later.

"Well, I just spoke to the hospital, and they say Mrs. Cay is still comatose," Grace said. "I feel so sorry for the Cays. Such nice people."

As Nancy nodded, a short, stocky man with curly red hair emerged from the back aisle of the pharmacy. "Okay, Gracie, that'll do it," he said in a loud, merry voice. "I just need you to sign off on this delivery and I'll be on my way."

Grace took the clipboard the round man held

out. "Oh, Nancy, this is Wayne Gast. He delivers for one of our distributors. Wayne, this is Nancy Drew."

Wayne thrust out a hand to Nancy and she shook it. "Good to meet ya," he said. Something about the man's wide belly and broad smile was so friendly that Nancy had to smile.

"Nancy has been checking up on Mrs. Cay," Grace said absently as she initialed the papers she held.

Gast looked baffled for a moment, then nodded. "Oh, the woman you told me about earlier," he said to Grace. "What a shame. Any word on her condition?" he asked Nancy.

"Nothing's changed," Nancy said.

Gast shook his head. "Sure hate to hear that," he said. He took the clipboard from Grace. "Well, I have to be on my way, folks. I'll see you in a day or two. My best to Mrs. Cay," he added as he strolled off toward the back door.

"Later, Wayne," Kevin Duffy called out.

"See ya, Wayne," a younger male voice called out. Nancy saw a tall, thin teenager poke his head from around some shelves and wave to the delivery man. Nancy guessed the guy was around eighteen. His long, straight dark hair was parted in the middle around a handsome, angular face.

"Hey, Eddie, this is my friend Nancy Drew," George said. "Nancy, this is Eddie Dubrowski. He's a clerk here part-time."

Eddie came out around the shelves, dressed in

baggy jeans and a loose striped shirt. "Nice to meet you," he said with a charming grin. "You're the brilliant mystery-solver, right?"

Nancy blushed slightly. "I try to solve some mysteries," she replied modestly. Over her shoulder, she noticed Kevin Duffy look hard at her when he overheard Eddie's words. It seemed to make him nervous to learn that she was a detective, she thought. She would have preferred that Kevin didn't know she was investigating the case, but there was nothing she could do about it now.

"Eddie just graduated from River Heights High this spring," George was saying.

"And I had to get right to work," Eddie said, rolling his eyes. "College doesn't come cheap these days." He leaned against the pharmacy counter, still fixing his winning smile on Nancy. "You know, you have beautiful hair."

George laughed. "Eddie, no one's safe from you!"

"Really, Eddie," Grace chimed in. "If you keep flirting with every woman who walks in here, we won't have any female customers left."

Eddie grinned. "I meant it, though," he said as he lifted a carton of baby powder. "Her hair is pretty."

Nancy smiled as Eddie walked off into the main part of the drugstore. Then she turned to Grace and lowered her voice. "Just one question before I go," she said. "Did Mrs. Cay ever have any kind of strange illness, Grace? Was she sick often?"

The smile dropped from Grace's face. She shook her head. "Mrs. Cay was hardly ever sick, and when she was, it was only a cold or flu. The strongest stuff she ever got here was a common antibiotic."

Nancy nodded. That was just what Don Cay had said. "Thanks, Grace," she said. "I'll stop by the hospital and let you know if I hear anything new."

The pharmacist thanked her. Nancy waved goodbye to George, then left the pharmacy area.

Nancy folded her arms across her white T-shirt, lost in thought as she walked down an aisle. As she neared the exit someone hurried past her aisle, knocking over a display of sunscreen. Nancy looked down toward the floor to see Kevin Duffy hastily picking up the plastic bottles. She suspected he'd been trying to avoid her.

"Let me help," Nancy said, thinking this would be the perfect time to get to the truth behind Kevin's secretive behavior.

"That's not necessary," Kevin mumbled.

Nancy put a bottle of sunscreen back on the cardboard display and looked Kevin directly in the eye. "Maybe you could answer a few questions for me before I go," she said, not waiting for his reply. "Why did you lie about being at Mrs.

Cay's? What were you doing there in the first place?" she pressed. "And how did you know that she was sick?"

"Not that it's any of your business," Duffy said slowly. "But I was checking up on Mrs. Cay because I knew she had a cold. And I knew she had a cold because I filled an antihistamine prescription for her yesterday."

Nancy was surprised to hear that Mrs. Cay had taken an antihistamine. She wondered if Don Cay knew this, or Dr. Volman. It was important information. Why hadn't Kevin revealed it earlier?

Just as she decided to use the pay phone in the foyer to call the doctor, the front door of the drugstore was forcefully flung open.

Nancy stepped back in surprise as Bess ran right into her. "Oh, Nancy!" she said in a shaky voice.

Nancy immediately saw the distress on Bess's face. "Bess, what is it?" she asked, worried.

Bess's lower lip trembled and tears came to her eyes. She grasped Nancy's hands tightly.

"My classmate . . ." she began in a shaky, whispered voice. "Regina's brother, DeWitt . . . He—he's dead!"

# 4

## *Cause of Death: Unknown*

As soon as the news about Regina's brother left her mouth, Bess burst into tears and collapsed against Nancy. "Shh," Nancy said soothingly as she gave Bess a hug. "Take it easy. Where did you hear this?"

"The teacher announced it in our class this morning," Bess said in a tearful voice. "Oh, Nancy, I just can't believe he's dead!" she cried, the sobs coming faster.

Nancy looked around. Customers in Twickham's were looking at Bess with a mixture of curiosity and compassion. "Bess, let's move out of the doorway," Nancy said gently. She walked Bess over to the pharmacy area. George, just stepping down from the pharmacy, stopped suddenly, looking at Bess in alarm. "What happened . . ." she began.

"Is there some place we can sit down privately?" Nancy said quietly.

"The bookkeeper isn't in today—we can use her office," George said at once.

She led them up through the pharmacy into a tiny back cubicle, where Bess sank down on a padded swivel chair in front of a paper-filled desk. She sat quietly, wiping her tears with a tissue and breathing deeply until she could speak.

"DeWitt Houser died," she finally told George.

George's mouth dropped open. "What?" she said in disbelief. "Regina's brother? The guy in your class? But how? When?"

Bess twisted her trembling hands in her lap. "DeWitt worked the early morning shift for a parcel delivery service," she said. "He never showed up for work this morning. One of his coworkers called his apartment but didn't get an answer, so he went over there. And . . . and he found DeWitt in his apartment . . . dead," Bess said. Tears sprang to her eyes again.

"What was the cause of death?" Nancy asked.

Bess shrugged. "They don't know yet."

"But he was so young," George said, sounding dazed. "He was a perfectly healthy twenty-year-old. How could he just die suddenly like that?"

Nancy frowned. She had to agree with George. "I can't help thinking," she said somewhat reluctantly, "he must have died from unnatural causes—like being the victim of a crime."

"No one would want to hurt DeWitt," Bess protested. "He was the friendliest, most caring person. He was popular with everyone at school."

Nancy nodded, but she privately refused to dismiss the possibility of foul play. She was determined to find out more.

"Does Regina know?" George asked Bess.

Bess sighed. "When I phoned her at work, they said she'd been called away by an emergency. I assume that the emergency was about DeWitt." She looked at her friends sadly. "I just can't imagine how she must feel."

Nancy was patting Bess's shoulder when a voice behind her made her jump.

"Oh, dear, I'm so sorry," Grace's clear voice rang out. Nancy turned to see Grace, Kevin, and Eddie peeking in the doorway of the small office, their faces serious and subdued. "We didn't mean to eavesdrop, but I was worried about Bess," Grace said. She slipped into the office and gave Bess a comforting hug.

As Grace released Bess, Nancy saw a strained look on the pharmacist's face. "DeWitt was a customers of ours," Grace added. "I knew his sister looked familiar to me this morning." She slid her hands into the pockets of her white lab coat.

"Two customers in one day," George added in

an odd tone of voice. She and Nancy traded glances, and Nancy knew George was thinking the same thing she was. Could there be some connection?

"Can you believe it?" a loud, jolly voice suddenly came from the pharmacy. "I left my sunglasses here again. I'm telling you, I'd lose my head if—"

Wayne Gast's round, smiling face appeared in the doorway behind Grace, Kevin, and Eddie. "Hey, what are you all doing in here?" he asked.

Grace stepped over to Wayne and softly told him the news. The red-haired man's face fell. "Oh, mercy. I only came back to look for my sunglasses," he said apologetically.

"I'll get them," Grace offered, and she and Wayne went back into the pharmacy.

Nancy glanced at Kevin Duffy, who was still hanging around by the doorway. He had been staring at her, but when their eyes met, his eyes shifted and he looked around uncomfortably. Finally, he silently backed away and returned to his station in the pharmacy. Nancy couldn't help wondering if Kevin Duffy knew something more about DeWitt Houser's death.

As the doorway cleared, Eddie Dubrowski hesitantly stepped into the office. His hands were thrust in his pockets and his handsome features were drawn together in concentration. "Um, did . . . uh, did you hear how DeWitt died?" Eddie asked. "I mean, the person who found him—could he tell anything by the position of the body, or something?"

Bess shuddered. "I have no idea," she said. "I don't even want to think about that."

"Oh, I understand," Eddie said quickly. "I just wondered if it was an accident, or if someone broke in, or . . . or I don't know," Eddie faltered. He looked at Bess again. "Had DeWitt been involved in anything dangerous lately?"

"What a thing to ask!" Bess said. She shook her head. "I'll let the police worry about that."

Nancy's detective instincts perked up. She had to admit, she herself had just been wondering about the possibility of foul play. But why would Eddie Dubrowski think that DeWitt had been involved in something underhanded? Looking at Eddie, Nancy saw that his easy manner was completely gone. He seemed awfully anxious to get information.

"Oh, yeah, I'm sure the police will look into it," Eddie said, almost to himself. He stood in the office doorway, seemingly lost in thought.

Nancy turned to Bess. "Why don't I take you home?" she suggested. "I'd like to stop by DeWitt Houser's apartment to see what the police have learned, but I can drop you off on the way."

Bess crumpled the tissue in her hand. "Oh, Nan, can I go with you to DeWitt's apartment?" she begged. "I couldn't stand sitting at home, not knowing what's going on." Nancy nodded.

George said, "I'll go, too, Nan. None of the deliveries I have are emergencies. Besides, I'm sure Grace wants me to find out what happened to DeWitt."

Eddie cleared his throat. "And then you can fill me in. Okay, George?" he said, trying to sound casual.

George shrugged. "Sure thing," she agreed. The three girls made their way out of the pharmacy, stopping only for George to check with Grace.

Outside, they all blinked in the bright noonday sun. Nancy and Bess swung around the corner to get Nancy's car, still parked at the coffee shop. Nancy turned to look for George.

She saw George bending over something on the asphalt of Twickham's parking lot. George straightened up and ran to Nancy and Bess, holding a small white card in her hand.

"What's that?" Nancy asked.

"Looks like a business card from some lab supply company," George said, reading the card. "Someone must have dropped it." She slid the card in the front pocket of her jeans. "I'll give it to Grace as soon as I get back," she added.

Bess gave George directions to DeWitt's apartment and George trotted over to the delivery car. Nancy and Bess walked on down the street to climb into Nancy's blue Mustang.

About fifteen minutes later, Nancy pulled into the parking lot of a large apartment complex, a sprawling collection of wood-shingled buildings. Nancy spotted George pulling the delivery car into an empty space in front of the building marked D. A couple of police cars and a small crowd of curious people were gathered in front of the building.

Nancy parked the Mustang, and she and Bess jumped out. They caught up to George, and then the three girls walked into the small glass-walled lobby of the multilevel building. Bess pointed the way up some carpeted stairs to the second floor.

A buzz of voices greeted them on the second floor. A few uniformed police officers, a police photographer, a couple of women in business suits, and some casually dressed neighbors stood singly or in groups in the hallway. A few stared at Nancy, Bess, and George as they made their way toward the open apartment door near the end of the hall.

As the girls approached, one of the police officers turned around. He was tall and lean, with an almost bald head. "Well, Nancy Drew," he said in a soft but deep voice. "I should have known I'd find you somewhere like this."

"Hi, Sergeant Benson," Nancy said, recognizing the River Heights police officer from other cases she'd worked on. She introduced Bess and George to Sergeant Benson. He looked carefully at Bess's tear-stained face and drew Nancy aside. "Is she a friend of Houser's?" he asked.

Nancy nodded. "She's a friend of his sister's,

and she was in a class with DeWitt," Nancy explained. "We heard that DeWitt was found dead by a coworker this morning, but we don't know the circumstances."

"We don't know it all yet, either," Sergeant Benson said. "We've got a couple of officers in his apartment now, searching the place."

Nancy nodded, twisting her neck a bit to try to peek in the doorway. "The medical examiner is here, too, looking over the body," Sergeant Benson added.

Nancy looked up sharply at the police officer. She drew back from the door, her mouth set in a grim line.

George stepped toward Nancy. "What is it, Nan?" she asked with a note of concern.

Nancy swiftly pulled George and Bess away from the doorway and drew them several steps down the hall. "Sergeant Benson says the medical examiner is here," she said in a low voice.

"So?" Bess asked. "Isn't that standard police procedure?"

Nancy shook her head, her eyes dark with concern. "No," she replied heavily. "They only call in the medical examiner if . . ." Her voice faltered for a moment, then she drew a deep breath.

"If the medical examiner's here, that tells us one thing," Nancy declared. "DeWitt's death may have been . . . a homicide."

# 5

## *A Hunt for Clues*

Bess's lower lip quivered. "Nancy, what do you mean?" she whispered hoarsely. "You're not saying DeWitt was . . . was murdered?"

Nancy held Bess's arm. "We don't know that yet," she said calmly, trying not to alarm her friend. "But they called the medical examiner here pretty quickly. That usually means there's something suspicious about the death."

The blood drained from Bess's face. "It can't be," she protested. "He didn't have an enemy in the world. Unless . . . unless someone broke into his apartment or something."

George put her arm around her cousin. "As Nancy said, we don't know anything officially yet," she said in a reasonable tone of voice. "Let's not assume the worst."

From the corner of her eye, Nancy saw someone walk out the front door of DeWitt's apartment: a middle-aged woman with blunt-cut dark hair, wearing a tailored pantsuit. The woman pulled surgeon's gloves from her hands and began to talk to Sergeant Benson. Nancy knew the woman had to be the medical examiner, and she sidled over to try to pick up on their conversation.

"What's the story, Dr. Baird?" Nancy heard Sergeant Benson say quietly.

The medical examiner shook her head. "It's very strange," she answered. "There are almost no marks on his body. The position of his neck, arms, and legs makes it seem that he suffered convulsions before he died. The tongue was bitten several times, and he must have fallen backward on his head." She gripped her bag. "I'll see what I can find out when the body is taken to my examining room, and I'll order the lab to rush me an analysis of his blood." She nodded at Sergeant Benson and walked away down the hall.

Nancy turned quickly so Sergeant Benson wouldn't catch her eavesdropping. She could feel her heart pounding. DeWitt might have had convulsions—just like Mrs. Cay. Was that just a coincidence? Suddenly, all her suspicions were on full blast.

Hearing voices behind her, Nancy turned to see two detectives in sport coats leaving DeWitt's apartment. One held a black briefcase, the other a large plastic bag with smaller plastic bags inside. Nancy recognized these as evidence bags, holding items that might be significant to the case.

The detectives moved aside to speak with Sergeant Benson. As the three huddled in quiet conversation, Nancy looked around quickly. She knew she was violating police procedures, but this was probably her only chance to inspect DeWitt's home. In two quick, silent steps, she moved to the open doorway.

The detectives and Sergeant Benson, standing against a side wall, didn't even glance her way. Nancy swiftly glided through the door.

DeWitt's apartment was small but quite modern. She stood in a tiny entry, with a living room in front of her and a kitchen to her right. A doorway in the middle of the right wall of the living room probably led to the bedroom, Nancy guessed. The far wall had sliding glass doors, leading out onto a balcony.

She stepped into the narrow white-tiled kitchen. Newspapers were scattered across a small wooden table, and a pizza box sat on top of them. Nancy lifted the lid to see two cold slices inside. A few dirty dishes lay in the sink. Nancy's eyes scanned over the many postcards stuck to the refrigerator door with magnets.

Suddenly, she heard Sergeant Benson's voice call out to someone in the hallway. She hurried into the living room, determined to get a quick look before the police returned. The room had bare hardwood floors, a plaid couch, a roomy easy chair, and a wooden desk. Nancy stepped toward the desk, still listening for voices behind her. She glanced over a stack of magazines on an end table and another stack of magazines and papers on the desk, careful not to touch anything. A memo pad on top of the desk had the words *To Do* written in pen across the top and a few lines scrawled beneath it. Nancy squinted at the messy handwriting. "Ask supervisor about switching routes next week," read the first item on the list.

Nancy figured the entry must have something to do with DeWitt's job at the parcel delivery company. She wondered why he'd wanted to switch routes. Had he run into some sort of trouble on his route?

A bump against the ceiling made her jump. Even though she knew it was just coming from the apartment above, she was anxious not to be caught snooping around. Turning away from the desk, Nancy strode over to the sliding glass door, silently opening it with the bottom of her T-shirt so she wouldn't leave fingerprints. She stepped out onto the small wooden deck.

There was only enough room on the balcony for a couple of lawn chairs and a little barbecue grill. But pots of flowers sat on the railing, alongside a watering can and a narrow box of herbs. A pile of gardening stuff—weed killer spray, plant food, a spade—sat in a corner by the wall.

Nancy stared at them for a second, jogging her memory. Then she remembered—she'd seen a can of that same weed killer this morning at Mrs. Cay's house. She stared at the green-and-black can. Pest-Off was the brand name. It might just be a coincidence, but she knew a good detective didn't overlook anything.

She stepped back into the apartment and carefully closed the sliding door with her shirt again. Suddenly a voice cut across the apartment. "Who let you in here?"

Nancy whirled around to see one of the detectives, a short, stocky man, glaring at her. She hesitated. She'd entered the apartment so quickly, she hadn't even thought up an excuse. "No one. I was just looking around," she said lamely.

"Who are you?" the detective demanded.

"Nancy Drew!" a low voice boomed from the doorway. Nancy looked behind the detective to see Sergeant Benson. "You know this area is off-limits," the police officer said.

Nancy crossed the living room. "I know," she said calmly. "I'm sorry."

Sergeant Benson turned to the police detective. "It's okay, Marty, I know her," he said. The detective gave Nancy a final glare as she passed by him and out of the apartment.

Sergeant Benson followed Nancy out to the hallway. "What are you trying to do?" he demanded, sounding irritated. "Marty Riegart is a strict detective. He goes by the book. I could get suspended for not blocking the doorway."

"I am sorry, Sergeant," Nancy insisted. She did feel badly about possibly getting the officer in trouble, but at least she had gotten a look around DeWitt's apartment.

Just then Benson looked over her head, and Nancy turned around and followed his gaze. "Hey!" he said to a man in the doorway. "Don't you go in there!"

Nancy saw a newspaper photographer trying to aim his camera into the apartment. As Sergeant Benson hurried over to deal with him, Nancy let out a deep breath. She was off the hook for now.

Turning around, Nancy saw George and Bess halfway down the hall, standing on either side of Regina Houser. Regina's head was lowered to her chest and her shoulders were shaking.

Nancy went to join them and gave Regina a long hug. "I'm so awfully sorry," she said quietly.

"Thanks, Nancy," Regina said in a choked whisper. "It's like a nightmare. I just spoke to him on the phone last night. He sounded so normal. He'd just gotten back from the writing lab at school—he'd been working on a paper. I reminded him of our family cookout next weekend."

"DeWitt hadn't been ill?" Nancy asked softly.

Regina shook her head. "He was in great shape," she said. "He loved all kinds of sports."

Suddenly a beeping noise cut into their conversation. George reached down to her jeans pocket, where a small beeper was clipped. She looked at the number and said, "It's a call from Twickham's." She glanced up and down the hallway. "I'll see if I can use a phone in a neighbor's apartment." She strolled down to a woman standing in a doorway, watching the police activity. They chatted for a second, then the woman led George inside her apartment.

Just then Sergeant Benson came up to Nancy. She moved away from Regina and Bess to talk to him. "Now, Nancy, promise me you won't try to sneak inside again," he said, trying to sound stern.

"I promise," Nancy said. "But I thought you should know I did notice one thing in there."

The sergeant raised his eyebrows.

"DeWitt had some plant food and weed killer out on his balcony by the flowerpots," she told him. "Well, this morning George and I witnessed a woman having respiratory trouble and convulsions. She had also been working with the same weed killer—Pest-Off. Do you think there's a connection?"

Sergeant Benson frowned. "It does look as if DeWitt had been having convulsions," he admitted. "I'll mention this to the detectives and make sure they took samples of the plant stuff on the balcony. Maybe you're on to something. Weed killer has some deadly chemicals in it, you know."

Then Sergeant Benson moved over to speak to Regina. "Ms. Houser?" he said. "I'm Sergeant Benson. I spoke to your parents earlier, but I didn't get a chance to introduce myself to you. I just wanted you to know how sorry I am. We'll do everything we can to figure out what happened to your brother."

Regina managed a smile. "That's very kind of you, Sergeant. Thank you," she answered.

Just then, Nancy saw George come back out into the hallway. She signaled Nancy aside to talk to her. "I have to make a delivery," George said. "Some girl got a bad case of poison ivy and Grace wants to rush some medication to her." She waved a piece of notepaper. "Do you know where Glen Oaks Drive is? That's where this Vanessa Heschel girl lives."

Nancy nodded and gave George directions to a new subdivision in River Heights.

"Thanks," George said. "Let me know if you hear any news about DeWitt." She hurried to the stairs and ran down them, disappearing from view.

Nancy rejoined Regina, Bess, and Sergeant Benson. "It's funny how you piece together an idea of a person from searching his stuff," the officer was saying to Regina. He held up several papers in his hand. Nancy recognized them as the papers that had been lying on the top of DeWitt's desk.

"For example, here's a roster of the kids that were on the basketball team DeWitt coached," Sergeant Benson went on. "With his job and class and everything, he still found time to help out younger kids. He really seemed like a nice guy."

Nancy, reading the paper over Sergeant Benson's shoulder, drew in her breath sharply.

"What is it?" Bess asked anxiously.

"Guess who played on DeWitt's team?" Nancy said. "Eddie Dubrowski—that guy who works at the drugstore with George."

"The one who acted so weird when he heard about DeWitt?" Bess asked. Nancy nodded.

"Eddie Dubrowski?" Regina repeated. "That name sounds familiar. I think I remember DeWitt mentioning him. . . ."

Then Regina's face went deadly pale. "Tell us, Regina," Nancy prodded her.

Regina looked at Nancy steadily. "DeWitt told me he cut a guy named Eddie Dubrowski from the team," she said. "And Eddie threatened to get back at DeWitt for it!"

# 6

# *A Deadly Coincidence?*

"Eddie threatened to 'get' DeWitt?" Nancy repeated, stunned. "You're sure it was Eddie Dubrowski?"

"It's a name that's easy to remember," Regina declared. "But DeWitt didn't think it was serious. He even laughed when he told me about it. He said Eddie had a bad attitude. He was always missing practice, but he got mad if he couldn't play. That's why DeWitt finally cut him."

Nancy nodded. Her thoughts were coming so fast they seemed to be running into one another. So that's why Eddie had acted so strangely when he heard the news about DeWitt. He had certainly been interested in what kind of evidence the police had about the death. It might mean nothing, but she would definitely have to ask Eddie a few questions.

Nancy turned to Sergeant Benson. "I think it's

time for us to go," she said. "Thanks again for your help." The police officer shook her hand, and Nancy and Bess headed for the stairs.

Outside in the sunshine, the girls both let out deep sighs. They were silent for a moment, and then Bess said, "Nan, if Eddie had argued with DeWitt, why didn't he tell us? Do you think he knows something about DeWitt's death?"

Nancy shook her head slowly. "I don't know. But his reaction makes me think he knows more than he's telling. We'll have to ask him about it."

"Now?" Bess asked.

"Not yet," Nancy said. "I don't want to leap to any conclusions. Maybe DeWitt's death was accidental." As they walked over to Nancy's Mustang, she filled Bess in on what she'd seen in DeWitt's apartment and what she'd heard the medical examiner say. "Maybe retracing some of his activities yesterday will tell us something," Nancy concluded as they got into her car.

"Regina said he had spent yesterday evening at the writing lab," Bess pointed out. "I have to go there anyway to start my paper—I could ask who saw DeWitt and what he was doing last night."

"Great," Nancy said. "Meanwhile, I can call the pizza delivery place and check out DeWitt's order from last night. And I have to call Dr. Volman and tell him about the antihistamine Mrs. Cay took. Maybe she was allergic to it." Nancy filled Bess in on her earlier conversation with Kevin, then said, "I should also do some research on this weed killer angle. My dad has some medical books at home I can look through."

"Why don't I meet you there in an hour?" Bess suggested. "We can have lunch and plan our investigation."

Driving away from DeWitt's apartment complex, Nancy first took Bess to the Marvins' house so she could get her own car to go to the writing lab. Then Nancy went on to her house, a few blocks away. She went straight inside and down the hallway to the cozy, book-lined library.

Stepping through the doorway, she stopped short at the unexpected sight of her father sitting at his desk. "Hi, there," Carson Drew said, crinkling his blue eyes as he smiled at Nancy.

"What are you doing home?" Nancy asked.

"I've been doing some research for a new case," the attorney explained. "I figured I'd have lunch here and look at some of my medical books."

Nancy perked up with interest. "What's the case about?"

Nancy's father shifted a large book from his lap onto the desk and leaned forward. "A former employee of a pharmaceutical firm, Branson-Flagg, is suing the company for wrongful firing," Carson explained. "The employee, Arturo Garcia, believes the company uses faulty research procedures. He claims he was fired for trying to do things according to standard safety regulations. I'm defending Branson-Flagg. Garcia thinks the company conducted sloppy tests because they were hurrying to get products on the market before their competitors. In addition to suing for the paychecks he believes he deserves, Garcia wants to blow the whistle on what he claims are careless safety policies that could harm the public."

Nancy scrunched up her face in thought. "The name of that company, Branson-Flagg, sounds familiar," she commented.

"I'm sure you've seen it on labels," her dad said. "They make all kinds of products, everything from soaps and hand lotions to specialized medicines for rare diseases." He started to collect his notes into a neat pile. "And what brings *you* home on such a bright sunny day? Another mystery?"

"How'd you guess, Dad?" Nancy replied. "But this is one I'm not too happy about." As she sat down and told him about Mrs. Cay's mysterious illness and DeWitt's death, she saw his blue eyes grow sober.

"You think the cases are connected?" he asked her when she'd finished.

"Maybe it's just a coincidence," Nancy said, "but both of them seem to have had similar convulsions."

"A twenty-year-old guy and an elderly woman," Carson Drew mused. "What could they have in common?"

"The only thing I've found so far is that both

did some gardening," Nancy said. "And both had Pest-Off weed killer in their homes. I thought I'd check it out in your medical books, in the section on poison?"

Carson gave her a sharp look. "Poison?" he asked. "You think these two people were poisoned?"

"Let's hope it's accidental poisoning, Dad," she softly replied.

"Well, good luck," her father said, giving her a pat on the knee as he stood up. "I need to get back to the office. I'll see you tonight." He gave Nancy a kiss on the cheek and left the library.

Nancy first picked up the phone on the desk and called Dr. Volman at the hospital. He was busy on his rounds, so she left a message for him to call her as soon as possible. Then she called Napoli Pizza, the place whose name had been on the pizza carton in DeWitt's apartment. Luckily, the guy who answered had been on delivery duty the night before. He remembered taking a small plain pizza to DeWitt's apartment. "Nice guy," he added. "He always gives decent tips."

"Did you notice if anyone else was there with him?" Nancy asked.

"Not that I could see," the deliveryman answered. "He looked like he was in the middle of studying or something."

Nancy took down the guy's name, just in case. Then she thanked him and hung up. Turning to her dad's shelf of medical reference books, she pulled out a couple of volumes on poisons.

She was soon so engrossed that she barely heard the doorbell ring forty minutes later. Hannah Gruen, the Drews' housekeeper, answered the door before Nancy could get up. A moment later she and Bess appeared at the door of the library.

"Bess says you haven't had lunch yet," Hannah said. "You two have work to do. Let me bring you a tray of sandwiches in here."

"Thanks a bunch, Hannah," Nancy said gratefully. Hannah had been with Nancy since her mother's death many years ago and was as close to her as any family member.

"What did you learn?" Bess asked Nancy, dropping down in a nearby armchair as Hannah left for the kitchen.

Nancy picked up one book and read aloud to Bess. "It says here that most poisons affect people in one of two ways," she said. "They're either absorbed through the skin, or they're ingested through food or liquids. Dr. Volman said that he thought Mrs. Cay might have ingested something, and that's what caused her reaction."

Bess nodded thoughtfully. "If it *is* the weed killer, how could that be ingested?" she asked. "It might get on your skin, but it would be pretty hard to swallow it, wouldn't it?"

"True," Nancy said. "But if it was around the

house, it could have gotten into something she ate or drank."

Bess's eyes widened. "But how could it get there—unless someone else slipped it in on purpose?" she said in a quavering voice.

Nancy grimaced. "I don't like that thought either," she said. "But remember, we're still not sure their symptoms were caused by poison. We'll have to wait until the hospital tests come back. What did you learn at the writing lab?"

"Well, DeWitt was there for about an hour last night," Bess reported. "He wasn't really writing a paper yet, just working out some ideas for his next one. DeWitt seemed to like running his ideas by other people. An instructor named Angela told me she talked with him about his paper."

"What about his mood?" Nancy said. "Did he seem nervous or in a hurry or depressed?"

Bess shook her head. "Angela said he seemed to be in a great mood," she replied. "She printed out for me a copy of what he was working on. I thought I'd read it over right now."

Nancy nodded, and the two girls each settled down to read. Nancy scanned the listings in a book describing various poisons. Each listing included the physical symptoms caused by the particular poison. Nancy hunted for something that might match Mrs. Cay's and DeWitt's reactions.

After several minutes and dozens of entries,

she suddenly sat up straight. "Listen to these symptoms, Bess," Nancy said. " 'Mild toxicity can produce nausea, stiffness of face and neck muscles, and other muscle twitching and contractions. More severe toxicity can lead to spasm, convulsions, interference with breathing, seizures, coma, and even death.' " She finished reading and looked up.

Bess met her eyes. "That sounds exactly like Mrs. Cay's and DeWitt's reactions! Which poison produces those symptoms?"

Nancy bit her lip. "Those are the reactions listed under strychnine poisoning," she said.

"Strychnine?" Bess asked. "Is strychnine an ingredient in weed killer?"

"I doubt it," Nancy said. "This book says that strychnine isn't used in much of anything. It's not something you'd have lying around the house. If you did, it would be clearly marked as a poison."

As Nancy sat thinking, Bess set aside the paper of DeWitt's she had been reading. "You should read this sometime, Nan," she said with a sigh. "Even though DeWitt was just jotting down ideas, he really knew how to tell a story. He wrote about the time his allergies flared up during a family vacation a couple years ago. It's very funny."

Nancy looked over at Bess. "DeWitt had allergies?" she asked.

"That's what he says here," Bess said. "They took this trip during hay fever season—the same time of year as right now. His suitcase fell off the top of the car the first day, with his allergy medication in it. Usually he took this antihistamine stuff every day. He tried to suffer along without it, but this was a camping trip, so they were outdoors—" Bess broke off. "What is it, Nan?" she asked.

Nancy stared intently at Bess. "Mrs. Cay was taking an antihistamine, too," she said. "She'd had a cold."

Bess shrugged. "Lots of people do."

"But lots of people don't have the kind of violent physical reactions Mrs. Cay and DeWitt did," Nancy said. She began talking faster as she became more excited. "If they were reacting to something they'd ingested, couldn't that something be a medication—like an antihistamine?"

"I guess," Bess said. Before she could say more, Nancy reached for the phone on the desk, quickly punching in a number. "May I speak to George Fayne?" she said. As soon as George was on the line, she spoke rapidly. "George, I need your help. Didn't you say that both Mrs. Cay and DeWitt Houser were customers at Twickham's?"

"Why, yes," George answered.

"Were both of them taking an antihistamine?" Nancy asked.

"Hang on," George said. "Let me check with Grace." She was gone for a few seconds, then came back on the line. Her voice now sounded low and strained. "Grace says they were both taking liquid Pandryl," she told Nancy. "It's an antihistamine that clears out sinuses and stops itching. Doctors prescribe it for colds and allergies and other things. Kevin filled the order for Mrs. Cay yesterday, and she picked it up herself. He filled DeWitt's prescription yesterday, also, and DeWitt picked it up. It's all here on the computer."

Nancy's heart started beating quickly. "George, what if both Mrs. Cay and DeWitt had a reaction to the Pandryl?" she said. "They were both taking it, and it looks like they had similar reactions."

George said gravely, "I thought of that as soon as you asked."

"We have to tell Grace not to fill any more prescriptions for Pandryl until we can check it out," Nancy said urgently.

"But, Nancy, it's too late," George exclaimed, her voice breaking. "That emergency delivery I had to make this afternoon—it was a bottle of Pandryl!"

# 7

## *A Triple Dose of Harm*

Nancy stifled a gasp. "George, where did you deliver the Pandryl?" she asked.

"To a girl named Vanessa Heschel," George said, sounding anxious. "She had awful poison ivy, and her doctor prescribed it to stop the itching. Oh, Nancy, what if she's already taken it?"

"Have Grace call the Heschels and tell them that Vanessa shouldn't take that medicine," Nancy said calmly and firmly. "If she's already taken it, tell them to get her to a hospital. And remember, we don't know if the Pandryl is responsible. Grace should say she's just recommending this as a precaution."

"Okay," George said.

"What's the Heschels' address?" Nancy asked.

"Twenty-three-fourteen Glen Oaks Drive," George answered promptly.

"Thanks," Nancy said, fixing it in her memory. "And, George, tell Grace and Kevin not to fill any more Pandryl prescriptions until we can check this out. And I'm afraid they'd better report this to the police, just in case."

George agreed, and Nancy hung up the phone. "Let's go," she said to Bess, jumping to her feet. "George already delivered some liquid Pandryl to a customer. We need to hurry over there and see if this girl's okay."

The two girls rushed into the hallway, just as Hannah came out of the kitchen with a tray of sandwiches. Grabbing one sandwich each, they said a quick goodbye to Hannah and ran out the door.

Nancy drove the Mustang quickly to the address George had given her. Soon she and Bess pulled up in front of a large, two-story gray house with a circular driveway.

The two girls hurried to the front door, where Nancy rapped the heavy brass knocker. Within seconds the door was opened by a short, slender man in a business suit, his tie loosened at the neck. He peered at Nancy and Bess from behind wire-rimmed glasses. "Yes?" he said.

"Mr. Heschel?" Nancy asked.

"Yes," he said. "Do I know you?"

Nancy smiled politely. "No, you don't," she said. "I'm Nancy Drew and this is my friend Bess Marvin. Did you just get a call from Twickham's?"

The man gave a short laugh. "I haven't gotten a call from anyone for the last hour," he said. "When you have two teenage daughters, the phone is almost always tied up—"

He stopped abruptly as they heard a loud groan, coming from somewhere inside the house. It was followed by a girl's voice crying out.

Mr. Heschel spun around, calling, "Vanessa? Vanessa!" He began to run up a carpeted stairway behind him.

Nancy quickly stepped through the door and crossed the entry hall to the stairs. Looking up the stairs, she saw a blond teenaged girl in a white bathrobe. The girl was hunched over, her arms clutching her stomach. Her legs buckled beneath her, and she sank down onto the top step as her father reached her side. "Vanessa, honey, what's wrong?" Mr. Heschel asked, obviously upset.

"I . . . I don't know," the girl said in a tearful voice. "I feel like I'm going to throw up. And my face muscles keep twitching."

Nancy turned to see Bess, staring in horror up at Vanessa. Suddenly George appeared on the front porch next to Bess. "Their line was busy," she panted, out of breath, "so I raced over!"

Nancy turned and sprinted up the stairs, knowing she couldn't lose a minute. "Mr. Heschel, this is what Twickham's was trying to call you about," she called out. "I think Vanessa may be having a reaction to the Pandryl they sent her."

Mr. Heschel gaped at Nancy. "What?" he said in confusion.

Nancy pointed to George behind her. "That's George Fayne. She delivered the medicine here an hour or so ago. She was trying to call you."

Mr. Heschel looked numbly past Nancy at George standing in the entryway.

Vanessa clutched her dad's arm. "I just took some of that stuff," she moaned weakly.

"There's no time to waste, Mr. Heschel," Nancy said, her voice growing urgent. "Vanessa must go to a hospital and get her stomach pumped."

Mr. Heschel stood up, his face drained of color. "I'll call an ambulance," he said, still sounding dazed. He trotted down the upstairs hallway to a phone.

Nancy crouched beside Vanessa. She could see the muscles in Vanessa's neck stiffening and her right cheek twitching. The girl gripped the step she sat on, her eyes terrified. As Nancy slid an arm around her shoulders, she could feel the girl's muscles going rigid.

Nancy's mind flew immediately to an image of Mrs. Cay's reaction that morning and she thought, Please, let us not be too late.

Nancy, Bess, and George stood in a waiting room at Rosemont Hospital, a new facility not far from the Heschels' house. Nancy was looking out the large window of the waiting room as Bess and George fidgeted on a fat-cushioned sofa nearby.

"Nancy, there is definitely something weird going on," George spoke up. "In one day, two of our customers are in the hospital and one is dead. It's got to be that Pandryl stuff. But what exactly is happening?"

Nancy sighed. She'd been trying to figure out the very same thing. "If those prescriptions *have* been tainted, then it sure looks like something strange is going on at the pharmacy," she said carefully.

George's nostrils flared. "Twickham's is the most reliable pharmacy in town," she declared hotly. Then, looking around, she lowered her voice. "If Grace found out anything funny was going on there, it would just devastate her," she said.

Nancy gave a slight nod, but she said nothing. She didn't want to upset George, but she couldn't rule out anything—or anyone. If it turned out that the Pandryl was tainted, then Kevin Duffy would have to be Nancy's first suspect—he had filled at least two of the prescriptions. Grace Cerrito would also have to be considered a suspect.

Needing to do something, Nancy picked up her purse and fished in it for some change. "I'm going to give Dr. Volman a call," she told Bess and George. "He may have been trying to reach me." She headed out of the waiting room and down the spotless hallway to a bank of phones.

She called River Heights General Hospital and eventually got through to Dr. Volman.

"I'm afraid I have nothing new to report," the doctor told Nancy. "Mrs. Cay hasn't regained consciousness yet."

"I thought you should know that the police have been investigating a death that was discovered this morning," Nancy said. "I heard that the dead man had symptoms similar to Mrs. Cay's—difficulty in breathing, muscle contractions. And I found out that both of them were taking a liquid antihistamine called Pandryl." Nancy took a breath. "Do you think the Pandryl could be the source of some poison? Or could they have been allergic to the medicine?"

"Well, Mrs. Cay *was* probably reacting to something she ingested," the doctor replied cautiously. "And Pandryl sounds like the only unusual thing she's ingested lately. You may be on to something here. I'll order a toxicology screen on Mrs. Cay. We'll run a whole series of tests on her, to see if there is anything strange in her blood."

Nancy thanked the doctor and hung up the phone. She leaned against the wall, trying to think things through. If the medication had been laced with poison, how many people could be affected? Was it the whole supply of Pandryl, or just the stock at Twickham's?

Was someone at Twickham's responsible? She

ran through the Twickham's staff in her mind. There was Kevin Duffy, who'd showed up at Mrs. Cay's house that morning without an explanation. She wondered again what the assistant pharmacist was hiding. Why hadn't he mentioned filling the Pandryl prescription earlier? And why didn't he want his boss to know he'd gone to Mrs. Cay's to check up on her?

Then there was Eddie Dubrowski, she remembered. Eddie's grudge against DeWitt Houser sure made him look suspicious.

But what connection did either guy have to Vanessa Heschel? she asked herself.

With a sigh, Nancy headed back down the hallway to the waiting room, reflecting that she still had a lot of investigating to do.

In the doorway, she almost ran into Bess and George. "They said we could see Vanessa now," Bess told Nancy. "They moved her from the emergency room to an outpatient recovery room."

The three girls set off at once for one of the small recovery rooms down the hall. There they found Vanessa lying propped up in bed, looking tired and pale. Gathered around her were her father, a woman who looked like her mother, and another blond girl, who Nancy guessed was her sister.

"Come in, please," Mr. Heschel said to Nancy and her friends. After everybody was introduced all around, he added, "I owe you girls a big thank you. The doctor said Vanessa was lucky to have gotten here so quickly. They pumped her stomach and flushed out whatever was causing that terrible reaction."

"Now, what is this about the Pandryl being poisoned?" Mrs. Heschel asked.

"I don't know for certain that it is poisoned," Nancy said quickly. "So far, three people seem to have had similar reactions, and all three were taking Pandryl." Knowing the Heschels were still shaken, she didn't mention that one person had died.

"Do the police know about this?" Mr. Heschel asked.

"Yes," Nancy said. "The pharmacist at Twickham's has informed the police. But it's still only conjecture—they'll need more information from the doctors, from the lab tests, and from the victims before they can confirm anything." She turned to Vanessa. "You can help by telling us—how much of the Pandryl did you take?"

"Not very much," Vanessa said. "Maybe just a teaspoonful." She managed a grin at Bess and George. "I went for a hike this morning with some friends and tromped right through a clump of poison ivy. By the time I got home, I was covered with red blotches. First I put on some anti-itch lotion, but that didn't help a lot, so we called my doctor and he prescribed the syrup."

"Had you felt queasy at all before you took the Pandryl?" Nancy asked.

Vanessa shook her head. "I felt great," she said. "I mean, I was itching like crazy, but I wasn't nauseated. And my face wasn't doing that weird twitching thing." She shuddered.

"Had enough excitement for one day?" a cheerful voice said from behind Nancy. A young, smiling woman with red hair, freckles, and a white lab coat marched up beside the bed. "Vanessa, I'm Dr. Lehane," she said. "I took care of you in the emergency room. How are you feeling?"

Vanessa looked up at the doctor. "Okay," she replied. "Still a little weak, though."

"That's normal," Dr. Lehane said. "You probably won't feel like eating anything too soon. Just start out with some mild foods when you feel ready."

"Doctor, do you know what caused Vanessa's reaction?" Mr. Heschel asked.

The young doctor shook her head. "We'll have to wait until the contents of her stomach are analyzed," she said.

"Gross," Vanessa's sister said.

Nancy turned to the doctor and explained her suspicions about the Pandryl, describing the two other possible cases. "Dr. Lehane, do you think the Pandryl could be poisoned?" she asked.

The doctor thought for a moment. "Vanessa's reactions are certainly consistent with strychnine poisoning," she admitted. "But strychnine isn't very common. I know it's used as a rat poison—in med school we used it to kill laboratory rats after experiments. But it's such a strong poison, it's rarely used commercially."

Dr. Lehane put her pen back in her pocket. "I'll ask the lab to put a rush on Vanessa's test results," she added. "But I sincerely hope you're wrong."

"Me, too," Nancy said. But deep down, she was beginning to think that she wasn't.

The doctor left, and the three girls said their goodbyes to the Heschels. "What now, Nan?" Bess said when they were back in the hallway.

Nancy sighed. "I hate to intrude, but I think we need to stop by the Housers' home," she said. "I'd like to see if there's any news on DeWitt."

Bess bit her lip and nodded. "Let me call them first," she suggested. "It's close to dinnertime."

Nancy nodded. "Tell them we'll only bother them for a moment."

"And I should call Grace," George said, "to update her about Vanessa. I know she was worried."

After a stop at the pay phones, the girls trooped out to the hospital parking lot. Nancy and Bess got in the Mustang, and George followed them in the delivery car.

Nancy followed Bess's directions to the Housers' home. They lived in an older, ranch-style house a couple of miles from DeWitt's apartment. Several cars were parked in the driveway—friends and relatives who'd come to console the family, Nancy guessed.

The three girls went to the door, and Nancy rang the bell. Soon it was opened by a red-eyed Regina. "It's good to see you," she said, sounding truly relieved. She lowered her voice. "I know all of these relatives mean well, but it's a little overwhelming. I keep having to describe DeWitt's last days, over and over again."

Regina opened the door wider to invite them in, but Nancy held back. "Regina, I don't want to upset your folks with a lot of questions," she said gently. "I just wanted to know if you'd heard from the medical examiner's office yet."

Regina looked quickly over her shoulder and then stepped out onto the porch herself, pulling the door almost closed. "We just got a call from them a little while ago," she said. "They know what must have killed DeWitt."

She paused and swallowed. "There was poison in his blood," she reported grimly. "Strychnine."

# 8

## *Some Poisonous Thoughts*

"Strychnine?" Nancy repeated. "Are you sure?"

Tears filled Regina's eyes. "That's what the medical examiner's office said. But how could DeWitt have strychnine in his blood?"

Nancy said grimly, "I think the antihistamine he was taking was contaminated."

"The Pandryl?" Regina said in disbelief.

"It's possible the prescription was tainted somehow," Nancy said. "But I don't have any proof. I'm sure the police will check DeWitt's apartment thoroughly, now that they know it was strychnine. They should find something soon."

"But why DeWitt?" Regina said, almost in a whisper. "Why would anyone poison him?"

"Two other people have had similar reactions to the Pandryl," Nancy told her. "So it may not have been intended specifically for DeWitt." But even as she said that, Nancy couldn't help thinking of Eddie Dubrowski's angry threat to DeWitt.

Nancy reached out to hug Regina. "I promise I'll do everything I can to find out," she said. Bess and George hugged her, too, and then the three girls left.

As they walked back to their cars, George said, "I've got to head back to Twickham's and check in. There are probably deliveries piling up."

"Let's all go there," Nancy said. "Like it or not, I'm afraid it looks like that's the center of this mystery."

"Unless a whole batch of Pandryl was contaminated somehow before it got to the drugstore," George said. Nancy could tell her friend was determined to believe that no one at Twickham's was guilty.

"It's possible," Nancy said. "At any rate, we should start at the beginning, tracing the path of the medication to each of its victims. And to do that, we'll need Grace's cooperation."

With Nancy and Bess in the Mustang and George in the delivery car, they headed downtown, stopping briefly to pick up hamburgers at a drive-in. They ate them in the car as they drove on to Twickham's.

As they entered the drugstore, it was obvious that something was going on. In the pharmacy, Grace, Kevin Duffy, and Wayne Gast, the distributor's deliveryman, were huddled around Kevin's computer, staring intently at the screen.

Behind them, Nancy could see two men examining the shelves of medications. She knew they were probably police detectives.

Grace caught sight of the three girls and hurried over to the pharmacy counter. "Not long after I called the police to report Vanessa's reaction, these detectives showed up," she said in an undertone. "They told me what the medical examiner said about DeWitt—that he'd been poisoned. And they think the strychnine may be in the Pandryl." She shook her head miserably. "It's a nightmare."

Nancy looked past Grace to see the detectives taking a large plastic bottle from the shelf. "They're impounding your Pandryl?" she asked.

Grace nodded. "Not just ours—they're taking Pandryl out of all the pharmacies in River Heights," she said. "And they're issuing a nationwide alert, just to be safe. What if an entire batch of this syrup is contaminated? Who knows where it could hit next?"

"Let's not panic," Nancy reminded her. "The police have to check every lead, and the Pandryl is one of them. Of course they have to be extra cautious."

Her words seemed to calm Grace a little, but they didn't do much for her own fears. Everything seemed to point to the worst conclusion, Nancy thought silently. If the medicine *was* contaminated, it could affect thousands of people!

She looked back at Grace. "What about your other customers?" she asked. "Are there more people taking Pandryl?"

"Kevin's searching our computer files to find who has had it recently," Grace said. Nancy, Bess, and George came around the counter and joined Kevin and Wayne Gast at the computer.

"It looks like just two others have gotten it in the last week, Grace," Kevin said tensely. He tore a sheet from the computer's printer and handed it to her. Then he stepped down to the front counter to wait on a customer. Nancy tried to catch his eye as he passed, but he avoided her glance.

Grace looked at the two names on the sheet. "I never dreamed I'd have to make this kind of phone call," she said unhappily as she reached for her phone.

"Can I help?" Nancy offered. "I could call the second person on another line."

"Good thinking," Grace said, tearing the piece of paper in half and handing the bottom to Nancy.

Nancy stepped around Wayne Gast to the pharmacy's other phone extension. The deliveryman held up two fingers, crossed for luck. Nancy nodded as she punched in the phone number for a customer named Sandy Bernard.

After several rings, a female voice answered impatiently, "Hello?"

"Is this Sandy Bernard?" Nancy asked.

"Yes," the voice said. "Who's this?"

Nancy could hear the sound of a child crying in the background. "My name is Nancy Drew," she said. "I'm calling from Twickham's pharmacy. I see that you recently got a prescription for Pandryl."

"Oh, yes, the antihistamine," Sandy said. "Uh-oh. I paid for it, didn't I?"

"Yes, of course. I'm not calling about that," Nancy said. "I wanted—"

"Not that it matters," Sandy went on. "I didn't use it—I never even opened the bottle. Wouldn't you know, as soon as I went to the doctor and got a prescription, the cold started to clear up on its own."

"Well, that's good news," Nancy said, her shoulders relaxing with relief.

Sandy laughed. "Well, it sure is good not to be sick anymore," she said. "But it was kind of a waste of time and money."

Nancy explained that the medicine was being recalled. She told Ms. Bernard not to take the medicine under any circumstances, and to return the bottle of Pandryl to Twickham's for a refund. Sandy Bernard promised to drop it off right after dinner.

Nancy hung up the phone and turned anxiously to Grace. The pharmacist was bent over, concentrating on her conversation. Finally she hung up and looked up wearily. "Well?" she asked Nancy.

"Sandy Bernard never took the Pandryl," Nancy announced.

"Mr. Riede did," Grace said. "Fortunately, he says he always takes a tiny first dose of any medication. He says he's sensitive to certain chemcials. As soon as he took the Pandryl, he threw it all up. He stayed in bed for twenty-four hours, and now he's feeling better. I told him we'd come by and pick up the Pandryl later."

The pharmacist sighed. "We're lucky he had such a mild reaction," she added. "Still, I advised him to call me if he feels the slightest bit ill." She glanced at the detectives behind her, and then lowered her voice. "But his reaction convinces me that there's something wrong with that Pandryl. What else could it be?"

"Let's not jump to any conclusions before the police lab has tested your supply of Pandryl," Nancy cautioned her. "Still, I have to admit—it looks bad. Maybe it'll help if we trace the path the medicine takes."

"Ask any questions you want," Grace said. "I'm more anxious to clear this up than you are. This drugstore's reputation depends upon it."

"I really doubt that the Pandryl was contaminated after it reached the customers' hands," Nancy pointed out reluctantly. "That would mean someone had to break into each customer's home, reopen the medication, and add the strychnine. And in Vanessa's case, we know George delivered the medicine less than an hour before Vanessa took her first dose. That wouldn't leave much time for someone to get to it."

Grace frowned. "Then that means something must have happened to the medication *before* it was sealed in the individual bottles," she said, meeting Nancy's eyes squarely. Nancy felt sure that Grace knew she herself was under suspicion.

Nancy met her gaze. "Where is the supply kept?" she asked.

"In a larger bottle in the pharmacy," Grace said. "As you can see, it's an enclosed area, not open to customers—just the pharmacists and the staff. Want me to show you how we fill a prescription?"

"Thanks," Nancy said. Glancing sideways, she noticed Kevin looking up from his computer, watching Nancy warily.

Grace tapped on her computer keyboard, and several lines of information came up on the screen. "We keep a computer record of every prescription," she explained. "We can tell where a customer lives, when his or her last prescription was, if there are any drug allergies, who filled the prescription, stuff like that." She moved the cursor on the screen. "We looked it up—Kevin filled both Mrs. Cay's prescription and DeWitt's. Oh, and you did Vanessa's, too, right, Kevin?"

Kevin looked up and gave a silent nod. Interesting, Nancy thought. Could it be coincidence that Kevin filled the prescriptions, or was it deliberate?

"How do you decide who fills a prescription?" Nancy asked Grace.

The pharmacist explained, "Kevin and I both answer the phone, taking down prescriptions that are called in from doctors' offices. Usually we have Eddie or the other clerk, Carl, at the front counter. When someone walks in with a written prescription, the clerk gives it to whichever of us looks least busy."

Behind Nancy, Wayne Gast's voice suddenly spoke up. "Most days, they're both working a mile a minute," he said. She turned to see him leaning against the shelves, wearing his usual friendly grin.

Grace managed a smile and then went on. "We verify the information on the prescription, and if everything looks okay, we fill it," she said. "First we go back to the shelves and find the supply bottle. For the Pandryl, we had a bottle that holds about a pint. You just pour out whatever dosage you need."

"Into what kind of bottles?" Nancy asked.

Grace reached beneath the counter and brought out a small, dark-colored glass bottle. "We pour the syrup into these," she said, "and then put a safety cap on top. These safety caps are so secure that a lot of customers can't even get them off. Then the bottle is either handed to the customer or put here in this box for George to deliver." She pointed to a shallow wooden tray at the end of the counter.

"So they could be sitting there for a while if George is out on a delivery run?" Nancy asked.

"That's true," Grace said.

"And what about these prescriptions?" Nancy asked, pointing to a wire basket on the counter, full of white prescription envelopes.

"Those have been filled but not yet picked up by customers," Grace said. "But they're kept inside the pharmacy area, where no outsiders can get them."

Nancy drew a careful breath. From Grace's explanation, one thing seemed clear. Anyone who worked in the drugstore had the opportunity to tamper with a medication—either in the supply bottle or after it had been filled, while it sat waiting to be picked up or delivered. That meant that Grace, Kevin, Eddie, and the other clerk, Carl, would be the police's chief suspects.

And George, too, she realized with a sinking feeling.

Nancy thanked Grace and left the pharmacy area. Lost in thought, she turned into an aisle and nearly fell over Eddie Dubrowski, unloading a box of shampoo onto a shelf.

Eddie looked up at Nancy. "Oh, hi," he said. Though he flashed Nancy a smile, he kept on placing each plastic container carefully on the shelf.

"Hi," Nancy said. She hesitated for a moment,

then decided to be direct. "I was at DeWitt Houser's apartment this afternoon," she said. "Now I understand why you were so upset about his death. He was your basketball coach."

Eddie froze in place, not looking at Nancy. Then he took another bottle from the carton. "Yeah. So what?" he said, looking at the shampoo.

"Were you on his team a long time?" Nancy said.

Eddie shrugged. "One-and-a-half seasons."

"Did you get along with DeWitt?" she asked.

Eddie's head whipped up and his eyes flashed at Nancy. "I argued with him, okay?" he spat out. "He always played favorites. He'd let the guys that were his little buddies play all the time, while the rest of us sat on the bench. I knew I was better than those guys playing, so I told him so. But he didn't care." Eddie gave a short, bitter laugh. "He said the problem was my attitude. Yeah, right."

Nancy looked at the handsome young man, slamming bottles onto the shelf. It was easy to believe that Eddie might have an attitude problem.

Suddenly Eddie stopped. "But I don't know anything about how he died," he said. "I may have been in a rotten mood that day he cut me from the team, but once I left the gym, I let it go. So you better look somewhere else if you want answers about his death."

That was strange, Nancy thought. She hadn't asked Eddie about DeWitt's death, yet here he was claiming not to know anything about it. She wondered if Eddie's conscience was bothering him.

Nancy shrugged. "I don't want what happened to DeWitt to happen to anyone else," she said. "We were lucky with Vanessa, but—"

Eddie bolted to his feet. "Vanessa who?" he asked, in a shocked voice.

"Vanessa Heschel, the girl who took Pandryl this afternoon," Nancy explained.

Eddie's eyes nearly bulged from his head. "Vanessa Heschel!" he yelled. "What happened to her?" he said, grabbing Nancy by the arm.

Nancy drew back, looking at Eddie in surprise. "I thought you'd heard," she said. "Vanessa had a reaction to the Pandryl, but we got her to a hospital, and—"

"What hospital?" Eddie cried.

"Rosemont," Nancy said.

Eddie took off down the aisle like a shot. Nancy spun around and watched him tear into the pharmacy, grab something near George's delivery tray, and head for the back entrance. Grace and Kevin stared after him, looking bewildered.

Then Nancy heard George, by the cash register, call out, "Hey! He took the keys to the delivery car!"

Nancy flew out the back door, with George at

her heels. As they tore out into the parking lot, the girls heard a squeal of tires.

Nancy grabbed George's arm and pulled her out of the way just in time. The delivery car sped past them, missing Nancy and George by inches.

Eddie Dubrowski was at the wheel.

# 9

## *Under Suspicion*

"What does he think he's doing?" George cried as Eddie swerved the delivery car onto the busy street beside the drugstore and sped off.

Nancy watched the car weave crazily away. "I might be wrong, but I think he's going to Rosemont Hospital," she said.

"Where Vanessa Heschel is?" George asked.

Nancy nodded. "I started telling him about Vanessa, and he just about jumped out of his skin," she said. "The next thing I knew, he was running through the pharmacy and out the door."

"Do you think he knows something about Vanessa?" George asked.

"He knows something all right," Nancy said. "But I'm not sure what. I talked to him about his fight with DeWitt, but he insisted he had nothing to do with his death. And then he took your car as soon as I mentioned Vanessa's name." She paused. "What do you know about Eddie?" she asked.

George shrugged. "He just graduated from high school," she said. "From what I gather, he was pretty popular. He always has girls calling him or guys stopping by the store to say hi."

"Is he in the pharmacy area much?" Nancy asked.

George thought for a moment. "I'm away on deliveries a lot, so it's hard to say," she answered. "He does go in there to help check in new stock or to take customers' prescriptions."

Nancy stared down the street where the delivery car had turned. Eddie's odd behavior wasn't proof that he was involved in the poisoning, she knew. She really didn't want to think he could do anything so horrible, but suspicion was bound to fall on everyone at Twickham's—including George. Nancy was determined to solve this case before things got nasty for her friend.

The two of them turned back into the drugstore, where they joined Grace and Bess in front of the pharmacy counter. "Well, what was that all about?" Grace asked.

"I'm not sure," George said. "Eddie just took off in the delivery car."

"I think he might be going to Rosemont Hospital," Nancy added. "When I mentioned that Vanessa Heschel was there, he was very upset. Do you know if he knows her, Grace?"

Grace rolled her eyes. "With Eddie, who can keep track of all the girls?" she said wryly.

"Have you ever had any trouble with Eddie?" Nancy asked.

"Oh, my, no," Grace said. "Sometimes he seems more interested in his social life than in work, but that's nothing new." She smiled a little. "I feel sorry for him. A lot of his friends are taking the summer off before they start college, but Eddie can't afford to. He's going to put himself through school, so he has to work. I think he's bitter about it, though he doesn't show it."

Nancy nodded, wondering just how bitter Eddie might be about working at the drugstore. Could his anger turn into something more dangerous—like tampering with medication?

Grace moved away from the girls to go back to work, and George went over to her corner of the counter. "I guess I'll straighten up. I can't make any deliveries without a car," she joked lamely. She began to stack up a pile of delivery receipts. "By the way, Nancy," she said, "that card I found on the ground in the parking lot this morning . . . where is it?" George stopped and frowned, her eyes checking the countertop. "I left it right here so I wouldn't forget to give it to Grace. I don't know where it's gone."

Nancy frowned and signaled to George. "Keep your voice down," she warned softly. "I don't know if that business card is a clue, but let's search for it without anyone noticing us."

While George leafed through her receipts, Bess wandered casually along the front of the pharmacy counter, searching behind bottles of vitamins and prescriptions waiting to be picked up. Nancy slipped up the step into the enclosed pharmacy, where Grace and Kevin stood at their computers, intent on their work. Nancy quietly walked behind the pharmacists, along the shelves of medications. Her eyes glided over every surface, looking for the card.

Just then Kevin stepped down from his work area to speak to a customer waiting for a prescription. Instantly, Nancy slipped over to his counter space. Behind his pill counter and computer, Kevin kept dozens of notes and reminders taped to the wall. There were small yellow notes, torn pieces of binder paper, and old prescription forms, all scrawled with tiny writing.

Her eye was caught by a framed picture tucked behind his computer—a photo of Kevin and a large golden retriever. Beneath the right corner of the frame, she spotted a familiar-looking white card. Sliding it along the counter, Nancy lifted it up and read Lampac Laboratory Supply.

She felt sure this was the card George had found. But why was it among Kevin Duffy's things?

Out of the corner of her eye, Nancy saw Kevin step back up into the pharmacy. She moved away from the counter, quickly sliding the card into her jeans pocket. She smiled brightly at Kevin as they squeezed past each other in the narrow pharmacy aisle. As he returned to his work area, Nancy left the pharmacy, joining George and Bess beside the cash register. She hid the card in the palm of her hand and showed it to them.

George nodded. "It's the same card," she whispered. "Where did you—"

Nancy hushed her with a quick look, then jerked her head toward the door to indicate they should go outside. Thinking fast, George gathered up the prescriptions on the lower counter. "Grace, I'll take my last run now, okay?" she said. "Nancy can drive me in her car."

Grace looked at her watch. "I guess you'd better do that. We close in half an hour," she said. "But where could Eddie have taken the delivery car? It's so annoying. I'd better give Rosemont Hospital a call and see if he's there."

Grace gave a half-wave to the three girls as they turned to leave the drugstore. As Nancy waved back, she reflected that Grace looked quite different than she had that morning. Her face was drawn and her small figure, which had filled the pharmacy with energy, now seemed listless.

Outside Twickham's front door, the girls paused. "The card was with Kevin Duffy's stuff," Nancy told her friends.

"Maybe he saw it on the counter and picked it

up," George said. "For all we know, he could have been the one who dropped it in the first place."

"Maybe so," Nancy said. "But as far as I'm concerned, it's another strike against him."

"You can't suspect Kevin," George protested.

Nancy gave her a level gaze. "Everybody at Twickham's is a suspect, George," she said solemnly. "I know you can't imagine that any of the folks you work with could be guilty, but that's where the evidence points right now."

George swallowed and looked away.

"Are we really going on a delivery run, George?" Bess asked wearily. "I was looking forward to getting home and taking a nice hot bath. I just bought some bubble bath that was on sale at Twickham's."

"We can drop you off first," George said. "You don't have to tag along on these deliveries."

Nancy looked over at the bank of pay phones at the gas station across the street. "First, let me call the number on this card," she said. "If Kevin Duffy went to the trouble of taking it, it may be more significant than we think. Can you wait for a minute while I use that pay phone?"

"Sure," George said. Nancy jogged across the street, and in a moment she was punching the toll-free number on the business card.

After a couple of rings, a voice came on the line. "You have reached the order department of Lampac Laboratory Supplies," it said. "We are sorry, but no one is here to take your call at this time. Please call back between the hours of nine A.M. and six P.M. Thank you."

Nancy hung up the receiver and stepped out of the phone booth with a frown. She still had no idea what Lampac did, only that whoever had dropped the card must have needed to do business with the order department.

She ran back across the street and told George and Bess what she had learned. The three then set off in Nancy's car, dropping off Bess at her home. Next Nancy and George headed to the southern part of town, to a couple of customers' houses that were close to each other.

Ten minutes later George was walking back to the car from the second house. She slid behind the wheel and picked up a small bag with a receipt stapled to the front. "This last one's a new one for me," she said. "Ninety-five Hunter Lane. I know where the street is, but I've never been to this house before."

George drove to the same neighborhood where Mrs. Cay's house was. It had become dark, and the streetlights had come on. Reaching Hunter Lane, George slowed the car, peering at the numbers on the houses.

Near the end of the block, the street became darker, with no streetlights or porch lights to guide them. "Is that it?" Nancy asked, her face pressed against the passenger window. "Ninety-five, was it?"

As George pulled hesitantly to the curb, they both stared at the dark, one-story house. There were no lights on inside, the lawn looked neglected, and the driveway was empty. They could just make out the faded numbers painted on a boulder near the door—95.

"Are you sure this is the house?" Nancy said. "It looks deserted."

George checked the receipt again. "Ninety-five Hunter Lane," she said with a shrug. "It's typed clearly. This must be it."

She grabbed the bag and stepped out of the car. Nancy watched uneasily as George picked her way up the concrete path, overgrown with weeds and strewn with leaves.

She saw George ring the doorbell and wait, bending sideways to look in the dark front window. After a couple of minutes, Nancy saw her knock several times on the front door.

Suddenly the front door swung open. George hesitated, and then Nancy saw her step into the dark house.

Without warning, George let out a hoarse cry. And in the next instant, Nancy saw her friend crumple onto the floor of the dark entryway.

# 10

## *A New Twist*

Nancy bolted from the passenger side of the car and raced up the walkway of the dark house.

"George!" she called, leaping up the two porch steps at once. "Are you all right?"

She heard a groan and stepped through the doorway. With a gasp, she saw George sprawled on the floor, a large wooden beam lying on top of her.

"I . . . I think I'm okay," George said. "I just have to get this thing off my leg. It really hurts."

Nancy stepped over George into the dark entryway. The thick piece of wood, about eight feet long, was lying over George diagonally. Nancy grasped the end and heaved it up. George slid her legs out and rolled to a sitting position.

Nancy set the beam down again. Dust flew as the wood hit the floor. "What happened?" Nancy asked.

George rubbed her leg ruefully. "The door must have been unlocked," she said. "It opened right up when I knocked. But there was no one here, so I walked in and said, 'Hello?' The next thing I know, I heard this scrape, and something hit my shoulder. I fell and this thing landed on top of me."

Nancy helped George to her feet. Then, while George brushed the dirt from her clothes, Nancy walked farther into the small, dark house. Only a faint light filtered in through dirty windows. Nancy saw no furniture in the front room—just spiderwebs, dust balls, and a pile of half-rotten boards.

Nancy sighed and returned to George. "I bet that beam was leaning against the wall," George said. "I must've knocked it over when I walked in."

"Maybe," Nancy murmured. "But what if someone put it there on purpose, expecting you to walk in?"

"Who would do that?" George asked uneasily.

"I don't know," Nancy said. "But someone called for a delivery to a deserted house. There must have been a reason. What if someone *wanted* to hurt you?"

"Why would anyone want to hurt me?" George asked gruffly, heading for the door.

"Maybe our culprit is afraid we're getting close to solving the mystery," Nancy said as they went down the path. "Or maybe . . . maybe somebody thinks *you* poisoned the drugs."

"Me?" George asked, incredulous.

"Anyone who works at Twickham's is a suspect," Nancy reminded her as they got in the car. "And you delivered Mrs. Cay's and Vanessa's prescriptions."

"But I'm not guilty!" George protested.

"I know that," Nancy said firmly. "But until we catch the real culprit, your name won't be cleared."

"Let's call Grace," George suggested. "Maybe she typed the wrong address on this receipt."

They drove until they found a pay phone, where George gave Grace a quick call. "Grace says that phone number is a disconnected line," she reported to Nancy when she got back from the phone. "The customer's name was given as Dave Oliver—a name she doesn't recognize. She says the order for the delivery was just phoned in this evening."

Nancy's mind raced as she started the car again. "Either one of the pharmacists could have easily engineered a phony delivery run," she mused. "And Eddie Dubrowski could have called in a phony delivery while he was away from the store."

George crossed her arms stubbornly. "Nancy, I'm positive none of those people would poison someone with strychnine," she said with conviction. "And anyway, if the Pandryl at Twickham's was contaminated, couldn't it have been someone who broke into the drugstore?"

"Grace would have noticed a break-in," Nancy pointed out. "Isn't there an alarm system there?"

George sighed. "Yes, there is. I'm sorry, Nan, but I just don't think Grace is involved in this crime. She's the most dedicated person I know. She worked with Martin Twickham for years, and he handpicked her to manage the pharmacy when he retired. Why would she start poisoning people?"

Nancy shook her head as they drove back to the drugstore. She hoped George was right. But she really didn't know.

The next morning, Nancy was sitting over a second cup of tea when the doorbell rang. She opened the door to find Bess standing on the porch. "Oh, Nancy, it was on the morning news," she blurted out. "The police are asking people to turn in any bottles of Pandryl they might have."

"I'm glad that people are being informed of the danger," Nancy said. "But now that the poisonings have been announced on the news, reporters will be snooping around Twickham's. That'll make our investigation that much harder."

"Have you learned anything new?" Bess asked, stepping inside the Drew house.

"I called Sergeant Benson this morning,"

Nancy reported glumly. "He told me that the lab found strychnine in the bottles of Pandryl that were sent to Mrs. Cay, DeWitt, and Vanessa—and in the large bottle of Pandryl in Twickham's pharmacy. I never found the bottle at Mrs. Cay's. Sergeant Benson said it was found in her pocketbook in a closet. She must have been planning to take the Pandryl with her when she went out. I also called Dr. Lehane," Nancy went on. "She said their lab confirmed that there was strychnine in Vanessa's stomach.

"I've just been reading up on strychnine," she added, holding up a thick medical book. "It says here that it's really powerful stuff. It often affects people within fifteen or twenty minutes of taking it. At that point, their faces and necks go stiff, and they could have convulsions and trouble breathing, depending on how much of the poison they ingested. A dose of five to eight milligrams could be lethal."

Bess shuddered. "I'll never forget that horrible look on Vanessa's face," she said. "We *have* to solve this case, Nan. But where do we go from here?"

"Could you go to Twickham's and try to talk to Eddie?" Nancy asked. "I want to find out why he reacted so strangely to the news of Vanessa's illness. I don't think he'll talk to me. He was testy with me yesterday. Use your charm on him."

"I'm sure he won't be able to resist," Bess said with a giggle. "But, Nan, do you really think

Eddie could be behind this? Was he that angry at DeWitt? And did he even know Mrs. Cay?"

"That's what we have to find out. Ask him about Mrs. Cay if you can," Nancy said. "I'll meet you at Twickham's in an hour or so, and you can tell me what you got out of him."

Bess said goodbye and bounced out the door. Nancy was just heading for the library to make some calls when her dad walked down the stairs, knotting his tie. "How's your new case?" he asked her.

Nancy briefly updated him on the latest developments. "The police asked everybody who has a bottle of Pandryl to turn it in," she mentioned.

"Pandryl?" Carson Drew asked, his eyes going wide. "The antihistamine syrup made by Wyandot?"

"Why, yes," Nancy said. "Have you used it?"

"No," her dad said, "but it's at the center of this case of mine I told you about. My client, Branson-Flagg, has been developing an antihistamine that won't make its users drowsy, which is a common side effect. Their big rival, Wyandot, was also testing a syrup like that, so they were racing to get it out. Wyandot got its syrup on the market first, and it's called Pandryl."

Nancy grabbed her father's arm in excitement. "Dad, do you think there's a connection between the Pandryl tampering and this rivalry between Branson-Flagg and Wyandot?" she asked breathlessly.

Her father considered the idea. "Lots of people at Branson-Flagg were unhappy when they saw Pandryl begin to make money," he said. "They felt that all of their hard work had gone to waste because they were just a little too late."

Nancy could barely stand still. "What if Pandryl bottles all over the country are poisoned and someone at Branson-Flagg poisoned them?" she said. "People everywhere could die!"

Carson Drew looked skeptical. "Branson-Flagg is a pretty reputable operation, from what I can tell," he said. "But even the best company could have a wacko working there. Branson-Flagg has a testing facility west of town. Arturo Garcia, the fired employee, was working there on the antihistamine. I've met the supervisor, Jerald Crouse. Why don't you talk to him?"

Nancy gave her father a hug. "Thanks, Dad," she said. "I'll look up the address and go there right now."

"Just be careful," Carson Drew said as he headed out the door to go to work. "And let me know what you find out."

A few minutes later, Nancy was heading to Twickham's. When she'd called Branson-Flagg to make an appointment, Jerald Crouse had sounded distinctly unfriendly, even though she'd told him she was Carson Drew's daughter. She had decided to get Bess and George to go with her to the Branson-Flagg testing facility, for support.

But as she neared Twickham's, her thoughts were interrupted by the backed-up traffic ahead. She peered forward and saw that a police officer was directing the cars into one lane. Then she looked at Twickham's parking lot. Vans from local television stations were parked bumper-to-bumper with police cars and other, unmarked cars. A police officer was posted at the front door of the drugstore, probably to keep out the reporters and cameras. She could only imagine how tense it was inside the store.

Nancy parked a little way down the street and walked up to the drugstore. Instead of going to the front, she headed through the parking lot to the back entrance. She was surprised to find the heavy metal back door unlocked. She knew it would be only a matter of time before the reporters found this other entrance, and she made a mental note to tell Grace to lock it.

Slipping through the door, Nancy found herself in the large back supply room, piled high with cardboard boxes. She stepped across the concrete floor, heading for the door that led into the main part of the store. As she did, she noticed that one side wall had an old wooden counter built into it. Invoices and papers were scattered across its worn surface. She figured this was where Eddie checked in new merchandise before putting it on the shelves.

Nancy moved closer to the counter, which was lit by a bare bulb hanging just above it. She glanced at the papers. Her heart skipped a beat when she spotted a small scrap of paper with a penciled scrawl that said, "Vanessa Heschel, 555-1652." She stared at the paper. Had Eddie written this?

Suddenly Nancy felt a hand roughly grab her shoulder from behind. "Who let you in here?" a gruff voice snarled.

# 11

## *Drive into Danger*

Nancy spun around to see Wayne Gast glaring at her, his usually happy-looking face twisted with anger. Nancy pulled away from his grasp. "I'm looking for Eddie," she said crossly.

Wayne's face instantly reddened. "Oh, it's you, Nancy," he said. "Gee, I'm really sorry. I thought you were another one of those news hounds." He jerked a thick thumb toward the front of the store. "They're like vultures out there. I had to fight through police cars and news cameras to make my delivery today."

Nancy smiled. "That's why I came in through the back—to avoid the crowd."

The red-haired man smiled back. "Smart girl."

"Hey, Wayne," a voice called from behind the piled-up boxes. "Is that you?"

Wayne Gast and Nancy turned around to see Eddie Dubrowski step into the lighted area near his desk. His expression darkened as soon as he saw Nancy.

"Nancy was looking for you," Wayne Gast said.

Eddie pushed his hair back from his face. "Don't tell me," he said wearily to Nancy. "More questions, right? Well, your friend Bess already covered everything. There's no need for you to snoop through my things back here."

"I didn't come here to snoop," Nancy said evenly. She slid a quick glance at Wayne Gast, who was simply standing there, drinking this all in.

"Why are you so suspicious of me?" Eddie asked, sullenly plopping down on the stool in front of his counter. "I don't know anything about this poisoner. All I know is that you've got to be pretty warped to do that to people. Besides, all of these drugs have safety seals and safety caps and extra wrappings. How could anyone contaminate them?"

A buzzer rang, and Eddie jumped from his stool. "Delivery truck," he said brusquely, moving toward the back door. "Gotta go unload."

Nancy stood still for a moment, thinking about Eddie Dubrowski. He had access to the poisoned Pandryl, and he had a bit of a motive for hurting DeWitt Houser. But what motive could he have had for hurting Mrs. Cay and Vanessa? And was he capable of committing such a horrible crime? Sure, Eddie had an attitude problem, but as he'd just said, a person had to be pretty warped to put strychnine in people's medicine. And Eddie just didn't seem that warped, as far as Nancy could tell.

Feeling Wayne Gast watching her curiously, Nancy turned and walked into the main part of the drugstore, with the deliveryman following her. As she neared the pharmacy area, Nancy could almost feel the tension in the air. The few customers the police had let inside were calmly browsing, but Nancy could see a worried look on Grace's face. When Nancy waved hello to her, Grace only smiled feebly.

She spotted Bess and George huddled in conversation by the cash register. Nancy walked over to join them, while Wayne went on into the pharmacy. "Oh, Nan, I tried talking to Eddie," Bess said, "but I didn't get much out of him. It was like he knew right away that you had sent me over here. All he told me was that he'd had a few dates with Vanessa a while ago, and they're still friends. He was worried about her when he'd heard she'd been hospitalized, and that's why he sped away in the delivery car."

"Did you feel that he was telling the truth?" Nancy asked her.

Bess shrugged. "He was pretty defensive," she said. "But then, everyone around here is on edge today. The police were here early, grilling everyone."

Nancy looked over at George. "Including you?" she asked.

George nodded, looking dejected. "They gave me a pretty rough time." George let out a shaky sigh. "Nan, I sure hope you solve this one soon. I don't like being a suspect."

"Don't worry, George, they have no evidence on you," Nancy said loyally. "The police aren't in the business of pinning accusations on innocent people."

Just then Nancy looked up at the pharmacy counter and saw Kevin Duffy staring intently at her. Something about the look on his face disturbed her. Then she remembered: It was the same look she'd seen at Mrs. Cay's house, when she asked him what he was doing there—a guilty, hunted, defiant look. As Kevin abruptly turned his tanned face away, Nancy wondered again if he could be the one responsible for the poisonings. He had access to the prescriptions and the Pandryl bottle, and he could have engineered that phony delivery the night before to the deserted house. And it was awfully suspicious that he was the one to fill all three of the tainted prescriptions.

Just then Grace stepped down from the pharmacy to join them. Nancy saw the same despondent look on her face as on George's. Clearly, Grace didn't like being a suspect, either. "Have the police found any other bottles of contaminated Pandryl?" Nancy asked the pharmacist.

"The other pharmacies in River Heights came up clean," Grace said. "Now they're checking other bottles manufactured in the same lot, in case that whole batch was tainted. Wayne was very helpful. He suggested they check Wyandot's distribution center in Center City, a couple of hours away.

"Wayne says that Wyandot isn't exactly known for its efficiency," Grace added. "He says he wouldn't be surprised if they got lazy with their safety inspections. I think the police are beginning to be suspicious of a problem at Wyandot. As you can imagine, that's a relief to me."

"As a matter of fact, I've been starting to think about the Wyandot connection, too," Nancy told the pharmacist. "My dad is working on a case now for Branson-Flagg—" She stopped when she noticed that Grace wasn't listening. Instead, she was staring across the drugstore at two men in plain dark suits who had just walked in the front door.

"Two more detectives," Grace said to the girls with a harried sigh. "Goodness knows what else they want, but I have to talk to them. Excuse me." She trotted off down an aisle to greet her visitors.

"What were you saying about your dad's case?" Bess prompted Nancy.

Pulling her attention away from Grace, Nancy described her conversation with her father that morning. "Dad says that Branson-Flagg has a testing facility just outside of town," she finished.

"I've made an appointment to talk to the supervisor. Do you guys want to come?"

"Sure," Bess said.

George straightened up with a groan. "I've got to get back to work," she said. "I have deliveries to catch up on. Grace was afraid that all the publicity about the poisoning would hurt business. But it looks as though our customers aren't all deserting us."

"That's good," Nancy said. "So do me a favor while we're gone. Between deliveries, try to keep an eye on Kevin Duffy." She glanced over again at the pharmacist, who was busy at his computer.

George looked at her quizzically. "Are you looking for something in particular?"

Nancy shook her head. "I just want to know if he does anything unusual," she said. "The same goes for Eddie." George nodded, and Nancy and Bess said goodbye and left the drugstore.

In a few minutes, Nancy was turning the car onto the highway that circled the city. She had lowered the roof on her convertible to take advantage of the warm, sunny day. As she eased the car from the highway to a two-lane road that would lead to the testing facility, she tuned the radio to her favorite station. Beside her, Bess leaned back in the passenger seat and closed her eyes, a contented look on her face.

Nancy pressed forward, thinking about what she wanted to learn at Branson-Flagg. She had been trying to figure out when the poison could have been added to the bottle of Pandryl at Twickham's. Could someone have sneaked into the pharmacy, unsealed the bottle, added poison, and resealed the bottle? Or had it happened after the bottle had already been opened?

Or maybe, she thought, the bottle was contaminated before it ever arrived at the drugstore. She frowned. It had passed through many hands from the time it was on some manufacturer's assembly line to its arrival at Twickham's. Did the rivalry between Branson-Flagg and Wyandot figure into this?

Deep in thought, she glanced in her rearview mirror. Though she had been alone on the road for the past few minutes, a van had now crept up behind her. It was going faster than she was, so she pulled over to the right shoulder of the road to let it pass.

Her eyes again flicked to the rearview mirror, wondering how close the van would get before it passed. The shoulder was narrow, and Nancy had to keep her eyes trained ahead and the wheel steady. She waited, expecting to see the van passing on her left.

Suddenly a dull thud made Nancy's blue Mustang lurch forward. Nancy and Bess were thrown forcibly against their seat belts.

The van had hit them from behind!

"Oh!" Bess cried, her eyes snapping open. "What was that?"

Nancy gripped the wheel tightly and steered back onto the road. "That van just rammed into us," she said, gritting her teeth. She checked the rearview mirror. The white van was so close that Nancy couldn't even see the driver, only the grill on the front of the truck. She sped up, hoping to shake the van from her tail.

"It hit us on purpose?" Bess said in disbelief, turning in her seat to get a look at the van. "I can't see who's driving. He's got this sunshade visor thing on his windshield. Who could it be?"

"I have no idea," Nancy said, intent on her driving. "But I sure don't like this kind of game."

Without warning, the convertible was again rammed from behind. "Whoa!" Bess said, drawing in a frightened breath. "What is going on?"

Nancy didn't know, but she was getting angry. Her car could have been shoved off the shoulder. Who was in the van, and why was this mystery driver out to get her and Bess?

Nancy clutched the wheel and floored the accelerator. The van began to speed up, too. She bit her lip, carefully judging the road ahead. The road cut through a hill, with rock ledges rising up fifteen feet on both sides. There was no place to pull over. "Hang on, Bess," she said in a low voice.

Nancy suddenly braked and swung her car around in a tight U-turn. With a squeal of tires, the Mustang neatly swerved into the opposite lane, heading in the other direction. The van sped past them, unable to make the same turn on such a narrow road.

"All right, Nancy! Way to go!" Bess turned around in her seat to watch the van. "It's going on at top speed," she reported. "I guess he decided not to try and follow us. Whew! I'd certainly like to know what that was all about. That driver could have killed us."

Nancy nodded grimly. "I get the feeling someone doesn't want us to go to Branson-Flagg's testing facility," she said quietly.

"Oh, Nan, you think that van was going after us deliberately?" Bess exclaimed, horrified.

Nancy turned the car around again to head in their original direction. "I don't think someone just playing around would actually hit us," she said. "After all, we could report this to the police. A person just fooling around wouldn't take that chance." She settled the car back into a regular speed on the two-lane road. "You didn't get the license plate number, did you?" she asked Bess.

"No," Bess said. "All I could see was a white blur. It was going so fast."

Nancy nodded. "I know," she said. "But I think there was some writing on the side of the van. I thought I made out a big letter *L*."

"An *L*?" Bess repeated. "Like maybe the first letter in the name of a company?"

"Possibly," Nancy said, slowing down a bit as

she approached an intersection. "My guess is that the van belongs to some company and—"

Nancy broke off. On the crossroad of the upcoming intersection she saw the white van—moving fast.

It was speeding right into the path of Nancy's car!

# 12

## *Weird Science*

"Watch it, Nancy!" Bess screamed from the passenger seat.

As the white van barreled toward them from the crossroad, Nancy jerked the wheel to the right, hoping the Mustang could speed through the intersection fast enough to get past the oncoming van. Her car swerved, bumping from the pavement onto the dirt of the shoulder.

From the corner of her eye, Nancy could see a flash of white pass just beside the convertible, coming only an inch from sideswiping Nancy's car. Quickly she turned the steering wheel back to its central position and slowed the car. She could hear Bess gasp as the Mustang just missed hitting a wire fence enclosing a field on the far side of the shoulder.

Braking to a stop, Nancy turned around and poked her head out of the convertible. The white van was careening down the crossroad, quickly moving out of sight behind the field. She squinted to make out the license plate number, but it was no use. The van was long gone.

She slid back down in the seat, feeling her heart still pounding in her chest. "Are you all right?" she said to Bess.

Bess's face was pale, but she nodded. "I'd just like to know who is so determined to keep you from investigating," she said in a shaken voice.

"That makes two of us," Nancy said. Who could have known where she'd be driving today, heading out to the testing facility? She'd talked about it with only her father and George and Bess. Had someone followed her from Twickham's?

She mentally ran through a list of folks from the drugstore: Grace, Kevin, Eddie. If any of them had left the store, George would have noticed it. Nancy planned to ask George about it when they returned.

She eased the car back on the road. "Are you sure you don't want to forget about this visit?" Bess asked hopefully.

Nancy shook her head. "We're almost there," she pointed out. "I'd hate to turn back. Don't worry—I think Mr. or Ms. White Van has quit for the day." She hoped she sounded more confident than she felt.

Bess was quiet for a few minutes, and then said, "I've been thinking about all this. Since the strychnine was found in the big supply bottle of Pandryl, that means the three victims were hit at random, right? They just happened to need that medication at the wrong time."

"That's true," Nancy said. "That almost seems worse than if they *had* been picked on purpose. Whoever is doing this doesn't even care who's being poisoned." She couldn't help but think of Mrs. Cay still lying helplessly in a coma in the hospital.

"It's like whoever it is doesn't have any conscience about it at all," Bess said, with a quiver of outrage in her voice.

Nancy nodded. "It's hard to imagine such a ruthless person," she said. Then, after a moment's thought, she added, "That does change our case in one important way. If the tampering is random, maybe we shouldn't look for someone who has any particular reason to hurt Mrs. Cay or DeWitt or Vanessa."

"That would mean Eddie or Kevin wouldn't be suspects," Bess said.

"Right," Nancy agreed. "Though I wouldn't rule them out completely. Still, maybe we should focus on someone who has a grudge against Twickham's or against the drug company, Wyandot. Both of them stand to lose a lot of business from this incident."

Bess pointed ahead to a large sign in the road directing them to the Branson-Flagg testing facility. "Well, here's one place we should find people who don't like Wyandot," she said as Nancy turned her car onto the winding driveway.

The testing facility was a modern-looking complex of four gray buildings, only a few stories high, with large, smoked-glass windows. The property was well landscaped, with trees surrounding the buildings and neat walkways between them. Everything looked tidy and spotlessly clean.

The two girls peered at a sign at the top of the drive, where arrows identified the various buildings. "Administration?" Bess guessed.

"I think we should try the Testing Center," Nancy said. She pulled the car into the lot of the nearest building and parked.

Nancy and Bess entered the building through smoked-glass doors. A blond woman behind a sleek black desk greeted them. A young man stood in back of her, scribbling on a large pad of paper.

"Can I help you?" the receptionist said in a professional voice.

"We'd like to see Jerald Crouse," Nancy said pleasantly. "I have an appointment. My name is Nancy Drew."

The young man behind the receptionist looked up. He also had blond hair, cut very short, and had a plastic identification tag clipped to his shirt pocket. "If you need to see Mr. Crouse, I could show you the way," he offered.

"Great," Nancy said. "Thank you."

He slid his pen back in his pocket and came around the desk. "I'm Brent Fielding," he said, shaking hands with Nancy and Bess. "I'm a lab assistant here, but my office is near Crouse's."

Brent Fielding set off down a gleaming empty hallway, with Nancy and Bess right behind him. After turning several more times into small corridors and climbing one flight of stairs, Nancy and Bess had both lost any sense of direction.

Noticing their looks of confusion, Brent smiled. "We call this building the Maze," he said. "We figure the design was some kind of joke of the architect's. You know, since scientists are always putting rats in a maze, the architect decided to put the scientists in one."

Bess and Nancy laughed politely at his joke. As they walked on, Nancy searched her memory. Where had she heard someone talking about laboratory rats recently?

Then she remembered. Dr. Lehane had mentioned that she had used strychnine to kill lab rats after experiments in med school. Nancy frowned. Did people at Branson-Flagg use strychnine for the same purpose in their experiments? If so, any employee here might have access to the poison.

She turned to Brent Fielding. "So what goes on here at the Maze?" she said, trying to disarm him with a smile.

The young man was leading them down a sterile-looking white hallway filled with large doors, most of them closed. "Well, we run stability tests and impurity tests on new medications," he said. "Before a product can be distributed to the public, it has to be thoroughly tested. Lots of studies are done on the medicines before they even get here. Then we take the extra precaution of seeing how a drug works over time, and under certain conditions."

Nancy nodded. "So you must be monitored pretty closely," she commented.

"Oh, yes," Brent said. "Anything that happens to the drug has to be documented, and anyone who works with it has to have his observations and research checked by several people."

He finally led them to a doorway that opened into a small cluster of offices. "Crouse's is letter *J*," he explained, leaving them at the door. Nancy and Bess thanked the young man and made their way across the carpeted corridor to an office with a small *J* tacked to it.

Nancy knocked on the closed door. A high-pitched "What is it?" came from the other side of the door.

"May I come in, Mr. Crouse?" Nancy called out.

"Door's open," the voice said sharply. She and Bess exchanged a quick look, and Nancy pushed the door open.

They saw a medium-size office with blank white walls and a few pieces of functional black metal office furniture. The one distinguishing feature of the room was the mass of papers piled everywhere—on the desk, on the file cabinet in the corner, and on the floor along the side walls.

In the midst of all the paper sat a slender man with short brown hair and a thin, wispy mustache. His complexion was pale and washed-out, as if the only light it ever saw was from the fluorescent light fixtures in the ceiling above him.

Without looking up, the man said, "Yeah?"

Nancy stepped up to the desk and put out her hand. "Mr. Crouse, I'm Nancy Drew, and this is Bess Marvin."

Crouse finally lifted his head from his work. Ignoring Nancy's hand, he stared both girls up and down with narrowed eyes.

"Who are you again?" he said in the same annoyed voice.

Nancy drew her hand back and took a breath. After the incident with the white van on the road coming here, she didn't feel like dealing with such a difficult personality. But she couldn't let Jerald Crouse's rudeness keep her from getting the information she needed.

"I'm Carson Drew's daughter," she said. "As you know, he's representing Branson-Flagg in a legal matter. I'm helping him investigate."

At the mention of a legal matter, Jerald Crouse pinched his mouth together and sat back in his chair, looking at Nancy suspiciously. "Well, don't think you're going to investigate *me*," he said. "I do things strictly by the book. Ask anybody here."

"I'm sure you do," Nancy said calmly. "But as my father explained, a former employee named Arturo Garcia believed that Branson-Flagg—"

At the mention of Garcia's name, Crouse let out a sharp, sarcastic laugh. "Oh, Garcia—I know all about him," he scoffed. "What a liar. The guy couldn't do his job, so he was fired. Now he thinks he can get money out of the company by claiming we're all sloppy. Hah! He'd better not get a cent."

"Well, that's why my father is defending Branson-Flagg," Nancy said smoothly. "But to build his case, he needs to know about the testing and distribution process—and especially how the antihistamine syrup Garcia was working on was proven to be safe. Perhaps you can show us how the process works."

Crouse sat up with a smirk. "Oh, right. Like you can just stroll through restricted laboratory testing areas, Ms. Drew," he said. "Listen, I can assure you that Branson-Flagg would never lower its research standards just to beat another company to the market. And we'd never release a product that we didn't stand behind one hundred percent."

"That's good to hear," Nancy said, "but—"

"In fact," Crouse went on, seemingly carried away by his anger, "if you want my personal opinion, Garcia was getting paid off by Wyandot, our competitors. Every time I'd recommend a procedure that would speed up our testing process or make it more efficient, he'd complain and try to stop me from doing it. I swear, he was deliberately dragging his feet. He was probably in cahoots with Wyandot the whole time."

Nancy looked puzzled. "But hasn't Wyandot's product, Pandryl, been found to be contaminated?" she pointed out. "Wyandot's reputation and business will be hurt by this poisoning incident. Won't that be a good thing for Branson-Flagg?"

Crouse nervously fingered his mustache. "This scandal will only show the public what a second-rate operation Wyandot is," he sneered. "I'll bet the contamination can be blamed on Wyandot and their carelessness."

"Such as?" Nancy said with interest.

"There are a million safety rules," Crouse said. "Around here, every batch of syrup has to be tested and documented, and every employee who comes into contact with the syrup has to be checked. Believe me, that's a lot of people."

Nancy nodded thoughtfully. She hadn't realized that drug companies followed so many safety precautions. "So it would be difficult to contaminate the medicine during the testing process, right?" she asked.

Crouse smiled. "Well, it could probably be done." Then, as though realizing he'd just said the wrong thing, he quickly added, "But of course, no one could get away with that here. I make sure that each pill, capsule, or syrup is never left to just one person's charge. Each person's work is checked by two others." He shifted his eyes toward Nancy. "But I can't vouch for Wyandot's procedures. Obviously, they're not as cautious as I am."

Nancy studied Crouse carefully. He was clearly anxious to have her believe that he ran a mistake-proof operation. But she wasn't so sure she could believe him. Why wouldn't he let Nancy view the testing operation, especially if it followed such high standards?

Besides, Crouse had just confirmed that there were bitter feelings between Branson-Flagg and Wyandot. Now he had admitted that there were ways to contaminate a medicine, even here. She'd sure like to find out more about Crouse and his supervising tactics.

Crouse seemed to sense her suspicion. He rose from his seat and opened his door. "That's all the time I can give you," he said abruptly. "I've got a lot of work to do. I'll show you out."

Bess quickly stood up and headed for the door. Nancy could tell Bess didn't like Jerald Crouse any more than she did. But Nancy didn't want to leave the testing facility yet. She still had too many questions.

As Crouse led the girls into the main hallway, Nancy lagged behind a few steps. Then she called out cheerfully, "I'll catch up in a minute. I think I've left my notebook in your office." She turned around, feeling Crouse's fierce stare on her back as she jogged back toward his office.

But as she reached Crouse's office doorway, she noticed a small, darkened room next to it. A sign on the door said: Absolutely No Entry. Property of Jerald Crouse. Violators Will Be Subject to Severe Penalties.

Nancy felt a flutter in her heart. Was Crouse working on some kind of secret project? Darting a glance over her shoulder, Nancy stepped inside the off-limits room.

The tiny lab had counters on three sides. On them sat papers, beakers, test tubes, charts, and unmarked glass bottles. Nancy took a step toward the counter to the right and tried to make out what was written on a pad.

Suddenly a voice came from behind her. "Get out of there now, Ms. Drew!"

# 13

## *Caught!*

With a gasp, Nancy spun around. Jerald Crouse had burst into the room. Bess almost banged into his back as she ran up behind him. Crouse's pallid face was red with anger.

"Ms. Drew, apparently you're ignoring the safety procedures I just spoke to you about!" he spat out furiously.

"But the sign on the door didn't say this was a lab area," Nancy said calmly. "What's in those beakers, Mr. Crouse?"

Crouse was still fuming. "The contents of those beakers is none of your business," he said. "You shouldn't be poking around in here."

Nancy gave Crouse a quizzical frown. "I didn't realize that Branson-Flagg allowed its employees to conduct solo experiments," she said.

Crouse eyed her, fingering his mustache nervously. "It's just a personal project of mine," he muttered, his fury suddenly drained away. "It's harmless. Please, just get out of here and don't touch anything."

Bess and Nancy both stared at Crouse, puzzled. He was acting awfully shifty, Nancy thought. "Is there something secret here?" she asked.

"N-no," Crouse said, his face reddening again. "It's just . . . well, as the sign says, it's private property." Then he shook his head impatiently. "Really, the two of you have caused enough trouble here. You must leave now."

Crouse grabbed Nancy's elbow, guiding her out the door of the tiny office and back into the main hallway. Without another word he led her and Bess back along the various corridors and stairs of the Maze, until they reached the reception area.

The receptionist looked up as they entered the lobby. Crouse suddenly put on a smarmy smile. "Thank you for visiting, ladies," he said in a phony, friendly voice. "I hope I've been helpful to you." Then he wheeled around and quickly strode back down the hallway from where they'd come.

Nancy and Bess walked out through the smoked-glass doors, still in a daze of disbelief. "Well, if that wasn't one of the strangest men I've ever met," Bess said once they were outside. "He practically dragged us from the building!"

"Truly bizarre," Nancy agreed. "He definitely

wanted us out of there. I don't think he wanted to talk to us in the first place, but he sure went nuts when I found that secret lab of his. It makes me wonder what kind of 'personal project' he could be working on."

"Do you think he has anything to do with the poisoning?" Bess asked as they reached the blue Mustang.

Nancy gave a thoughtful sigh. "I really don't know," she confessed. "His manner was certainly strange. He was so touchy about his procedures, even though he knew my father is defending Branson-Flagg. Maybe his testing process isn't as strict as he claims, or maybe he has something else to hide." She unlocked the car doors. "Or maybe he's just a weird guy."

"He obviously doesn't think too much of his competition, Wyandot," Bess noted as they climbed in the car.

"Right," Nancy said. "He even seemed kind of pleased that Pandryl was recalled because of this poisoning. After all, now Branson-Flagg can release its syrup and tell people that it's a safer choice." She frowned. More and more, it looked as though Jerald Crouse had a real motive for the poisoning.

"And he said he knew how you could contaminate a medication," Bess added.

"But that's what confuses me," Nancy said, pausing for a moment before starting the car. "If the strychnine was added to the Pandryl at a testing facility, then it would most likely end up in several bottles. But so far the only reported poisonings have been at Twickham's."

"Which brings us back to square one," Bess said. "But if the strychnine was added at Twickham's, who do you think did it?"

"Well, we know it wasn't George," Nancy said.

Bess gave a bitter chuckle. "Yeah, but the police don't know that," she said. "They told her they'd need her for further questioning, and they took her fingerprints and everything. It really upset her."

Nancy shook her head in frustration as she started the car. "That's one more reason for solving this case as fast as we can," she said, her jaw set in determination.

The two girls went on discussing the case as they drove back to River Heights, stopping on the way at a drive-in restaurant for a late lunch. But they seemed to be talking in circles. Nothing brought them closer to any kind of solution.

Both girls were tired by the time they reached the Drew house. They headed straight for the kitchen and found a large pitcher of iced tea that Hannah had left for them in the refrigerator. Filling their glasses, they sat down at the breakfast table. The trip to the testing facility had taken a few hours, and it was already late afternoon.

Nancy phoned River Heights General and Rosemont hospitals to learn that Mrs. Cay was still in a coma, but Vanessa had been released already. Nancy also called Chief McGinniss to see what the police investigation had turned up, but he wasn't in. She left a message asking him to call her back.

At a loss, the girls began to discuss what the next move in their investigation should be. "We need more background information on Kevin Duffy and Eddie Dubrowski," Nancy was saying, when the doorbell rang. She sprang up to answer it.

Nancy opened the front door to find George, leaning against the wall with her hands jammed in her shorts pockets. "Hey," George said listlessly. "I was hoping you'd be back by now."

"Are you in the middle of a delivery run?" Nancy asked her.

"No, I got off early," George said, stepping inside and following Nancy to the kitchen. "I had to go down to police headquarters for more questioning. Then Grace decided she's closing the store tonight at six. With all the uproar, it was hard to do business. So she told me I could go on home. How was your visit to Branson-Flagg?"

They lounged around the table while Nancy and Bess told George about their visit with Jerald Crouse. George sat listening silently. When Nancy and Bess had finished, she said, "Well, he sounds like a weird guy, all right. But I doubt that the poisoning took place at a testing facility."

"Why do you say that?" Nancy asked, perking

up. "Did something new happen while we were gone?"

"The police called Grace about an hour ago," George said. "They confirmed that only one bottle of the whole lot of Pandryl was contaminated. And that was the one at Twickham's."

"That clinches it," Bess said, sounding disappointed. "So someone was deliberately going after the people at Twickham's. Someone who wanted to ruin the drugstore's reputation."

"It could be that," Nancy said. "Or it could still be random. What if one bottle of Pandryl was poisoned and that bottle just happened to end up at Twickham's?"

The three girls sat frowning for a moment at that possibility. The poisoning victims were very real to them. It was hard to think of them as being just unlucky targets of a twisted, random act.

Nancy suddenly jumped up. "I know. Let's bake cookies! Maybe some chocolate chips would help us think more clearly."

"Sounds good," George said.

"You know I'm always up for eating," Bess chimed in.

Searching the kitchen, the girls found all the ingredients they'd need for the cookies. Nancy turned on the oven to preheat it, and soon the three of them were measuring flour, sugar, and chocolate chips. They were all glad to be concentrating on the physical tasks.

As George was greasing the cookie sheet, Nancy suddenly asked her, "The medicines that Wayne delivers to Twickham's—where does he pick them up from?"

George shrugged. "His company has a central distribution center. I think it's in Columbia City, a couple of hours away," she said. "He works for a place called Lang Distributors."

"Lang Distributors?" Nancy repeated. She looked at Bess. "Wasn't that the name on the side of the van that tried to force us off the road this afternoon?"

"What van?" George cried. "Who tried to force you off the road?"

Nancy explained about the run-in with the white van and that she and Bess never got a good look at the writing on the side of the vehicle. "And I meant to ask you, George, who was at the drugstore around noon time? Was anyone gone for more than a few minutes?"

"We were all gone at one time or another. Grace, Kevin, Wayne, and I all had to go to the station for questioning," George replied.

"So it could have been any one of the staff," Nancy mused.

"You said you saw a big *L* on the side of the van," Bess recalled. "That could be Lang."

Then Nancy's eyes popped open. She had almost forgotten about another supplier. She dashed to her purse, dug to the bottom of it, and pulled out the white card George had found in the parking lot at Twickham's yesterday. "Lampac Laboratory Supplies," she read. "That starts with an *L*, too. I think I'd better give them a call."

With George and Bess watching tensely, Nancy stepped to the telephone and dialed Lampac's phone number. The same recorded voice answered, "You have reached the order department at Lampac Laboratory Supplies. We are sorry, but there is no one here right now to take your call. . . ." Nancy felt her heart sink in disappointment.

Just as she was about to hang up, a real voice came on the line. "Hello? Can I help you?"

"Oh," Nancy said in surprise, "I thought you were closed."

"We're about to close," the female voice said. "But somebody turned on the recording too soon. I can still take your order if you'd like."

"Thank you," Nancy said. "I wanted to check on an order placed within the last few weeks." She paused, knowing that her hunch was a wild one. "It was an order for strychnine."

She could hear the clack of a keyboard. The woman said, "One moment, please . . . let's see. I have a couple of orders for strychnine. Would this be the one in River Heights?"

"Yes," Nancy said, her pulse racing excitedly. "That's the one."

"That order should have been shipped a couple of weeks ago," the woman said. "That's when it left our warehouse. Let me check that we got the address right." There was more keyboard clacking.

Then the woman's voice came back to the receiver. "Here it is. The customer's name on that order of strychnine was Wayne Gast."

# 14

## *The Culprit*

Nancy stared at the countertop in front of her, stunned into silence as the woman rattled off an address. "Ma'am?" the woman's voice said. "Was that the correct address?"

"Uh, yes," Nancy said. "You did say that the order was shipped, right?"

"Oh, yes," the woman assured her. "According to our records it arrived in River Heights a couple of weeks ago."

"Thank you," Nancy said. "You've been a big help." She hung up the phone and turned back to Bess and George.

"What is it, Nan?" George said anxiously.

Nancy's thoughts were racing ahead of her, and she shook her head, trying to clear it. "Dr. Lehane told us yesterday that she'd used strychnine to kill laboratory rats after experiments were performed," she said. "When we were at

Branson-Flagg, I wondered if the testing facility would have any strychnine lying around for the same reason. But someone could also easily order strychnine from a lab supply company, like Lampac."

"And did they?" George said.

Nancy slowly nodded. "Wayne Gast did, just a couple of weeks ago," she said.

George gasped. "Wayne? What on earth for?" Then both she and Bess looked at Nancy in horror. "Oh, no. Wayne is the poisoner," George said in a soft, shocked voice.

Nancy's face was locked in concentration. "I hadn't considered him a suspect until now," she said. "But it makes sense."

"I don't get it," George protested. "Wayne loves Twickham's. And he doesn't even know DeWitt or the other victims."

"This poisoning is random. It has nothing to do with the victims as individuals," Nancy said solemnly. "And Wayne just purchased strychnine. Why else would he do that? There aren't many uses for it anymore."

"Oh, Nan, do you think that was Wayne driving the white van this afternoon?" Bess asked with a shudder. "He could have killed us!"

"If he is our poisoner, he doesn't seem to care whom he hurts," Nancy said grimly. "Think about it. Working for Lang, he has access to all kinds of medications. He delivers products from Wyandot and other drug makers, right, George?"

George nodded.

"So at some point, he would have been alone with those bottles of Pandryl," Nancy continued. "At the testing facility, the drugs are checked by several people at once. At the drugstore, there is usually more than one person in the pharmacy. But when Wayne takes them from Lang to the stores, he's alone with them."

"Do you mean he opened a Pandryl bottle when he got them from the distributor?" Bess asked.

"I'm not saying anything for sure yet," Nancy said cautiously. "But he could have gotten the large Pandryl bottle from the shelf at the distributor's warehouse, opened it, added the poison, and resealed it. There would have been some kind of seal on the top of the bottle, but he might have been able to re-create that. Then he'd deliver it to the store, where the syrup from that bottle would be poured into smaller bottles for customers."

As Nancy spoke, she could feel herself becoming more excited. She couldn't believe she hadn't considered Wayne Gast before. He had greater access to the Pandryl than almost anyone. Yet everyone, including her, had been focusing on Twickham's or on the drug makers.

"But why would Wayne poison anyone?" George asked. "What would be his motive? Everyone likes him, and he seems to love visiting all the local pharmacies, especially Twickham's."

"I've been wondering the same thing," Nancy said, frowning as she thought of the friendly, overweight deliveryman. "How long has Wayne been delivering for Lang?"

"I thought I heard him say he started about nine months ago," George said. "Before that, he worked for some drug company as a research or technical assistant or something."

Nancy's eyes lit up. "Was it Branson-Flagg? Or Wyandot?" she asked.

George shrugged helplessly. "I really don't know," she admitted. "When he talked about it, I wasn't paying too much attention. It didn't mean much then."

Nancy quickly looked at her watch. It was past six already. Twickham's would be closed. "George, do you think Grace would mind if I called her at home?"

"Not at all," George said. "I have her number in my bag somewhere." She fished through her waist pack until she retrieved a torn piece of paper and handed it to Nancy.

Nancy hurriedly dialed the number as George and Bess waited tensely. The cookie dough still sat in the bowl.

Nancy could hear the weariness in Grace's voice as she answered. "Oh, Nancy, hello," Grace said when Nancy identified herself. "I hope you have some good news for me. I could use it."

"Well, it's more like a question," Nancy said.

"Could you tell me what Wayne Gast used to do before he began delivering for Lang?"

"Wayne?" Grace said in surprise. "Oh, let's see, I believe he worked for Wyandot in its research department. Why do you ask?"

Nancy ignored the question for the moment. "Why did he leave Wyandot?" she asked.

"They had a big series of cutbacks," Grace said. "Many people were laid off, and Wayne was one of them. What are you getting at?"

Nancy could feel her hands trembling with excitement. She couldn't believe it. Wayne Gast had worked for the company whose product had now been contaminated. And it was contaminated with strychnine, which he had purchased just a couple of weeks ago.

"Nancy, are you still there?" Grace asked.

"I'm sorry," Nancy said, snapping back to attention. "Tell me, Grace, did Wayne deliver that bottle of Pandryl to Twickham's—the one that was found to be contaminated?"

"I assume he did. He delivers most everything for Wyandot," Grace said. Then Nancy heard her draw in a sharp breath. "Oh, Nancy, you're not thinking that Wayne—" She stopped.

"How can we be sure he delivered it?" Nancy said, intent on collecting her evidence.

"It would be on the log-in sheet at the store," Grace said. "He and I both would have signed it. We do that for every delivery."

"Is there some way I can get a look at this log-in sheet?" Nancy asked.

"I'll tell you what," Grace said, a little spirit back in her voice. "I'll meet you at Twickham's in twenty minutes, and we can take a look at the sheet. And, Nancy, if you're looking for information on Wayne, you might ask Kevin and Eddie. They know more about him than I do."

Nancy thanked her and hung up. She turned to Bess and George. "Wayne used to work for Wyandot, in their research department," she said, trying to keep her voice calm.

"Oh, my gosh," Bess said. "So he must have known about the rivalry with Branson-Flagg over the Pandryl."

"I'm sure he did," Nancy said grimly.

"And he's always complaining about Wyandot, and how sloppy they are with their safety procedures," George offered quietly. She slapped a hand to her forehead. "I can't believe that I didn't even suspect that Wayne could be involved in this."

"None of us did," Nancy said. "But you know, we still don't have any concrete proof that he was involved. We need to gather some stronger evidence before we make any accusations." But even as she spoke, Nancy knew how anxious she was to find the poisoner and have him arrested. She couldn't help thinking about Mrs. Cay lying in a coma.

Grabbing the telephone book, Nancy located the listing for Kevin Duffy. She punched in the number while Bess and George took the book to look up Eddie's telephone number.

"Hello, Kevin?" Nancy said, hearing him answer the phone. "It's Nancy Drew. Sorry to call you at home, but I'm trying to get some information on Wayne Gast. I thought you could help."

"Wayne?" Kevin said, sounding confused. "Why do you need to know about him?"

Nancy paused, unsure about how much to tell Kevin. Finally, she said, "I've been trying to trace the bottle of the contaminated Pandryl. Wayne is naturally one of the links in the chain that brought the bottle to the drugstore." When Kevin didn't respond, she went on. "I know that Wayne just started delivering for Lang about nine months ago. How does he like his job?" she said, trying to sound conversational.

"I guess he likes it all right," Kevin said, his tone of voice still uncertain. "He's probably happier doing this than he was working for Wyandot. He still complains about that place. But he's had a rough time the past few months, with his mother and all."

Nancy blinked. "What about his mother?" she asked.

"She died a few months ago," Kevin told her. "I think Wayne took it pretty hard. They were very close. He still lived with her."

"How did she die?" Nancy asked.

"I'm not exactly sure," Kevin said. "I think she'd had a long illness, though."

Nancy nodded, thinking to herself that Mrs. Gast's death was significant, without knowing why. She thanked Kevin for his help and hung up. Then she reported the conversation to Bess and George.

Nancy figured she had time for one more call before going to meet Grace at the drugstore. She dialed the number George had found for Eddie Dubrowski.

Eddie's mother answered and called Eddie to the phone.

"Eddie, this is Nancy Drew," she said after he said hello. "Do you have a minute to talk?"

"More questions?" Eddie asked in an edgy voice.

"Just one," Nancy said. "And it's not even about you. I wonder what you can tell me about Wayne Gast."

"Wayne?" Eddie repeated, seeming as surprised as Kevin had. "He's always nice enough to me. Why?"

"Well, I'm trying to find out if he was having any difficulties with his job at Lang," Nancy said, trying to keep her explanation as vague as possible.

"Hmm," Eddie said, thinking. "I don't think he ever said much about Lang. Of course, don't get him started talking about Wyandot—you'll never hear the end of it. He hates that place!"

"Oh, really?" Nancy said.

"Yeah," Eddie said. "You know how he's always so friendly and happy? Well, anytime he talks about Wyandot he suddenly gets really angry. He rants and raves about everything they do."

"Is he angry about something specific?" Nancy said.

"I don't know," Eddie said. "To be honest, once he starts griping, I sort of tune him out."

"Mm-mm," Nancy murmured. She wondered to herself why none of the people who knew him ever thought his anger at Wyandot was suspicious. It was probably because of his happy-go-lucky demeanor. Maybe nobody had taken the deliveryman too seriously.

She thanked Eddie and hung up. "I'd better get going," she said to Bess and George. "But I'd like to ask Sergeant Benson about Wayne. Would the two of you try to call him while I run down to Twickham's?"

"What should we ask him?" Bess asked.

"See if the detectives learned anything when they questioned Wayne today," Nancy suggested as she stood up and grabbed her small purse. "And tell Sergeant Benson about our run-in with that white van today."

"No problem," George said.

Nancy flashed a smile. "I'll be right back," she promised as she headed for the door.

* * *

Only minutes later, Nancy was pulling her car into the dark, empty parking lot at Twickham's. As she jumped from the Mustang, she could see Grace already standing at the front door, her silhouette lit by a streetlight a few yards away. She waved to Nancy.

"Have you been waiting long?" Nancy asked, shivering a bit in the cool June evening. She noted that Grace had changed into jeans and a sweatshirt.

"Nope. Just got here, in fact," Grace said. She pulled a large ring of keys from her purse and began unlocking the series of locks on the drugstore's front door. "But let's hurry. I want to find that log-in sheet and make sure it was Wayne who delivered that Pandryl. If it was," she said firmly, "you'll have to tell me why you suspect Wayne is the poisoner. That's what this is all about, isn't it?"

Nancy nodded. "And while we're here, maybe I can ask you a few questions about him," she said, as Grace unwrapped a heavy chain and padlock from the door.

Grace pulled one of the doors open, sliding the bolt shut again as soon as she and Nancy had stepped inside the drugstore. The light from the front of the store illuminated the shelves near the store's entrance, but the rest of the store was dark. Nancy could hear the quiet purr of the refrigerated cases.

"The light switches are in the back," Grace explained, heading for the rear of the store. "I'll snap them on, grab the log-in sheet from Eddie's desk, and meet you back by the pharmacy."

Nancy nodded. She slowly groped her way to the pharmacy. As she got deeper into the store, it became darker and darker. Familiar as she was with the store when it was lit up, she couldn't help but feel it was spooky right now.

At that moment the lights in one half of the store blinked on. Nancy figured that Grace had hit the switch for only half of the store, since their search would take just a couple of minutes.

Reaching the pharmacy, Nancy stepped up to Kevin's and Grace's working areas. It was odd to see the usually humming computers and ringing phones sitting silent amid the stacks of papers, prescriptions, and empty medicine vials.

Standing at Grace's work station, Nancy absently leafed through the pharmacist's address card file. She came to Wayne's business card, where the address and phone number for Lang Distributors was printed. She gazed at it, noting that Wayne had even supplied Grace with his home number for emergencies.

Suddenly the drugstore went black. Nancy's head snapped up. "Grace?" she called out.

There was no answer.

Nancy glanced over toward the windows by the soda fountain, but they cast only a faint glow of light reflected from the street. "Grace?" Nancy called again. "The lights have gone out."

Again only silence answered. Grabbing the counter, Nancy felt her way, hand over hand, down the step to the cash register just in front of the pharmacy area. "Grace!" she called a third time.

A husky voice suddenly broke through the eerie silence and darkness. "I hope you're not thinking of going for the door," it said. "Because it's locked."

Nancy stood stock-still, aware of her heart beating.

She knew that voice. It was Wayne Gast's.

# 15

## *Trapped!*

Nancy didn't move. She could tell that Gast's voice was coming from about halfway across the store. She told herself not to panic, to breathe normally and listen for Gast. He probably knew the store's layout better than she did.

But what had happened to Grace? Nancy wondered. Had she met Gast in the back? Was she all right?

Then Nancy thought of the phones in the pharmacy. Turning from the cash register, she silently felt her way back up into the pharmacy. Standing in front of Grace's work area, she groped for the phone on the wall in front of her.

"Don't bother trying to use the phone," Gast's voice called out from across the store. "I've cut the lines, of course."

Nancy froze. Could he actually see her in the pitch-black pharmacy? She peered into the darkness of the store in front of her. She herself could see nothing. Maybe Gast couldn't actually see her, but had guessed she'd go to the phone. Not knowing, she ducked behind the counter, trying not to make a sound for fear that Gast might hear her, as well.

"You thought you were so smart, didn't you, Nancy?" Gast's voice rang out.

Nancy could feel goose pimples on her arms. Gast's voice, which she remembered as being jolly, was now deep and humorless. And he must have seen her if he was using her name. Nancy tried to figure out exactly from which part of the store the voice was coming. She had to find Grace and get out of the drugstore. She couldn't stay in the pharmacy area. If Gast cornered her there, she'd have no escape.

She crouched and slowly began to creep around the counter, down the step to the cash register.

"I don't know why you're so worried about a few people swallowing strychnine, anyway," she heard Gast say as she crept from the pharmacy area. "That's nothing compared to what Wyandot did to my mother. Killed her, you know—a long, slow death."

Nancy felt a chill run down her spine as she heard Gast's words. But she told herself to ignore him for now, and instead find an exit quickly. She recalled speaking to Eddie in the back room earlier in the day and thought she remembered seeing a small window there. If she could make her way back to that room, maybe she could crawl out the window.

Still crouching, Nancy headed toward the far corner of the store, where the entrance to the back room was. She moved slowly, afraid of bumping into something and letting Gast know where she was.

As she crept down an aisle that smelled like shampoo, she heard footsteps behind her and froze.

Gast's voice rang out, "Hey! I know you're moving around. Do you think I'm kidding? This gun is no joke." Nancy could hear the click as a safety catch was released from a gun.

She slid silently to the end of the aisle and turned left. Now she could smell the perfumes and lotions of the cosmetics section.

Then, without warning, a loud shattering noise cut through the silence. Just in front of her, bits of glass sparkled as they caught the dim light from the storefront. A heavy, sweet scent exploded into the confined air of the drugstore. Nancy clamped a hand over her mouth to keep quiet.

"Give it up now!" Gast yelled out as glass from many perfume bottles rained onto the floor and shelves. "I'm losing patience!"

Nancy could hear his voice moving away from her. He doesn't know I'm here, she thought. He must have shot at the perfume bottles at random, simply to scare her.

She began to creep forward, but her shoe found a small piece of the broken glass, crushing it. Nancy winced, hoping it wasn't heard.

"Oof!" Gast called out, and she heard his stumbling footsteps over by the pharmacy. He must have tripped on the step leading to the raised area.

Knowing he was far from her, Nancy scuttled furiously across the floor. In a moment she had reached the door to the pitch-black back room. Slipping around the doorjamb, she stood up in the back room, gratefully feeling the blood rush back into her aching back and legs.

But as she drew a breath, Nancy realized she'd still have to be careful back here. The room, she remembered, was full of boxes stacked high, and she didn't know where the walkways were.

She moved forward silently, making out the outline of Eddie's desk just at the entrance. Looking up, she caught a faint square glow of light near the ceiling. Her heart leaped a little. That had to be the window.

She stepped forward, keeping her hands in front of her to feel for any obstacles. Every sound she made seemed to echo in the silence. Slowly, she tiptoed to the back brick wall where the window was.

The window was about six feet from the floor. Peering upward in the filmy light, Nancy could see no lock on it. It was small, three feet wide and three feet tall at the most. Quietly setting a box in front of her, she stepped on the cardboard and reached for the hook at the top of the old window.

She could feel years of dust and dirt caked on the window frame. She pulled down, but the window didn't budge.

Gritting her teeth, Nancy gave the window a hard yank. The glass scraped open stiffly. She winced at the noise. Had Gast heard it?

But Nancy knew she didn't have time to find out. She pulled the window down until it hung completely open. The sound of cars driving by on the street outside was a relief.

Without wasting a second, Nancy grabbed the window frame and swung her right leg up and through it. Pushing off with her other leg, she ducked her head through the opening and pulled her body after it.

Just as her head emerged into the cool night, she felt a hand clenching her left leg. "Not so fast, Nancy," Gast snarled right behind her.

Nancy felt her heart drop. She had been so close! She tried to pull away from Gast's grip, twisting her leg and pulling her body outside.

But Gast held firm. As he yanked fiercely on her leg, Nancy felt herself slip backward again. Fighting tears of frustration, she struggled to hold on to the outside brick wall. The window frame cut at her leg as Gast's strong hand pulled her in the opposite direction.

Suddenly a flash of light filled the back room. A voice yelled out, "Police! Don't move, Gast!"

Wayne Gast dropped Nancy's leg and slumped back, looking stunned.

Nancy bent her head and looked inside to see that the lights had been flipped on. Two police officers stood in the door, training their guns on Wayne Gast. Just behind them Nancy spotted Grace, bound and gagged in a corner of the back room. One of the officers, hearing her thrash around, was just turning to find her.

Still teetering on the window frame, Nancy looked outside and saw George and Bess race around the corner of the building toward her. "Nancy!" Bess cried out. "Are you all right?"

Nancy shifted her body and dropped to the pavement below. George, reaching her side, wrinkled her nose. "Uh, you went a little heavy on the perfume tonight, didn't you, Nan?" she said.

Nancy giggled in relief. "I'll explain later," she said. "I'm just glad you guys got here in time."

"It took us forever to get through to Sergeant Benson," Bess said. "By that time, we figured you should have been home, Nancy. So we told him he might want to check things out here."

Nancy smiled at her friends. "Thank goodness you did."

* * *

As she stepped under the tinkling bell at Twickham's the next morning, Nancy couldn't help but feel that the bell sounded cheerier. She knew it was probably just a reflection of her own mood. She had slept better knowing that Wayne Gast was behind bars.

"Oooh! You can still smell that perfume," Bess said, behind Nancy.

"I think it'll be a long time before that odor goes away," Nancy said with a smile.

"Oh, Bess, I meant to tell you I spoke with my dad this morning. He received a call late last night from Jerald Crouse. Mr. Crouse actually apologized for the way he treated us. It seems that his department has been singled out for their safety practices in the lawsuit, and his job is on the line. He was just being doubly sure we didn't get our hands on something that could be dangerous."

"Well, I think he could have been a little more polite if he was so concerned for our safety," Bess remarked.

"I agree," Nancy said.

"The guy was definitely paranoid if you ask me," Bess continued.

Nancy laughed.

"You have a way of attracting some strange characters, Nancy, did you ever think about that?"

Nancy laughed again. "Goes with the territory," she said.

"But it sure does keep things interesting," Bess went on. "Now I've got a title for my creative writing essay: 'The Case of the Poisoned Pandryl.' "

The two girls headed over to the pharmacy, where Grace and Kevin were at their usual positions behind the counter. George stood in front, near the cash register.

"Good news, girls," Grace called out to the two girls. "I heard from Don Cay this morning. Mrs. Cay has come out of her coma, and she'll be fine. As you might expect, she's eager to get back to her garden."

Nancy felt her heart swell. "That *is* good news," she said. She looked up at Kevin Duffy, who was nodding in agreement. "You know," she said to Kevin, "I never did find out why you lied about being at Mrs. Cay's house the day before yesterday."

The pharmacist gave a sheepish grin. "I was just worried about her," he said. "The first prescription I ever filled here was for her, so I sort of consider her my personal customer. But we were so busy that morning, I didn't want Grace to know I'd left the store. When you saw me at Mrs. Cay's, Nancy, I panicked and I made myself look even worse by lying." He winced guiltily and looked at Grace.

"But you know I wouldn't have minded your leaving!" Grace protested, looking hurt.

"Well, after you'd just chewed me out about

the prescription count the night before . . ." Kevin's voice trailed off. "I didn't bring up the fact that Mrs. Cay took the Pandryl because I didn't think it would cause those symptoms. I knew she had no allergies because I checked her medical history before I filled the prescription. Not in a million years would I have suspected a deadly poison in one of my prescriptions!" He managed a smile and then turned to Nancy. "Anyway, I'm sorry if I was rude to you that day."

Nancy smiled. "Apology accepted."

"So, Nancy, tell us what happened with Wayne Gast," Grace said eagerly.

Nancy drew a deep breath and began. "Sergeant Benson called me this morning and confirmed what I'd suspected," she said. "Wayne Gast had worked for Wyandot on the Pandryl project, as a research assistant. About the same time, his mother, who was dying of cancer, agreed to participate in a test of some experimental drugs for Wyandot.

"Eventually Wayne was laid off, and he felt very bitter toward Wyandot," Nancy went on. "Then, a week later, his mother died. Medical records showed her cancer was already well advanced. There wasn't much that could be done for her, but Wayne blamed her death on the experimental medications."

"Poor guy—to have all that happen at once,"

Grace said. "No wonder he became unbalanced."

"So he figured he'd get back at Wyandot for his firing and his mother's death?" Kevin said.

Nancy nodded. "He hoped Wyandot would be involved in a big scandal," she said, "and lose millions of dollars and their reputation. He was so familiar with Pandryl, he figured he could easily taint that medication."

"I guess it didn't bother him that people could be hurt along the way," Bess said bitterly.

"How did he actually poison the Pandryl?" another voice said. Nancy looked up to see Eddie Dubrowski leaning against the pharmacy counter.

"First he got a job at Lang as a deliveryman," Nancy explained. "Then he took a bottle of Pandryl from the warehouse and brought it home. He opened the bottle, added the powdered strychnine he'd bought, and used his own wax and foil to reseal the bottle. He had seen it done at Wyandot, so he knew what a sealed bottle should look like."

"And then he delivered it here?" Grace asked.

Nancy shook her head. "Wayne told the police that he put it back in the warehouse with all the other bottles," she said. "It just happened to end up here. He said he had nothing personal against Twickham's."

"Nothing personal?" Grace repeated sarcastically. "It almost destroyed the store!"

"So it was Wayne who booby-trapped that abandoned house we delivered to?" George asked.

"Yep," Nancy said. "He told the police he'd noticed it during his delivery runs around town. He began to worry when he saw us poking around in the drugstore, so he called in a request for that phony delivery. Then he set up that beam to fall when someone walked in."

"I had the police check into the phone number for that delivery," Grace mentioned. "It turns out it was Wayne's mother's old number."

George frowned. "That's just gruesome."

"And when that didn't work, he tried to run us off the road in his van yesterday," Bess put in. "It's as if he has no regard for human life."

"You've got that right," Eddie put in. "I can't believe it. I never would have thought Wayne was capable of all this. He was lucky only three people got the tainted Pandryl."

"One question, Grace," George said. "Why did the three people who took the Pandryl have three different reactions?"

"Each one was prescribed a different dosage of the syrup," Grace pointed out. "So they each got different amounts of the strychnine. Mrs. Cay and Vanessa were lucky that people were around when they swallowed the poison, so they got medical attention quickly."

"I just wish DeWitt had been as lucky," Bess said sadly. "By the way, Nancy, I spoke to Regina this morning. She said to say thank you. She says just knowing who did this has helped her family."

Nancy nodded, glad she could do something.

Eddie quickly changed the mood of the conversation. "Well, one good thing has come of this," he said brightly. "Guess who I have a date with? Vanessa Heschel!"

Grace laughed. "So you visited her at the hospital, huh, Eddie?"

Eddie grinned and waggled his eyebrows. "I even brought her flowers," he said. "Turns out she'd always been more interested in me than she'd let on."

"What girl could resist your charms, Eddie?" Grace said teasingly.

"Well, she did have one condition when she agreed to go out with me," Eddie admitted. "She says she won't go hiking. She doesn't want to take any chance of catching poison ivy again."

Everyone laughed. "Smart girl," Nancy said.

"Smart, yes," Grace agreed. "But not as smart as our Nancy Drew."

# THE HARDY BOYS® SERIES By Franklin W. Dixon

| |  |  |
|---|---|---|
| ☐ | #69: THE FOUR-HEADED DRAGON | 65797-6/$3.50 |
| ☐ | #71: TRACK OF THE ZOMBIE | 62623-X/$3.50 |
| ☐ | #72: THE VOODOO PLOT | 64287-1/$3.99 |
| ☐ | #75: TRAPPED AT SEA | 64290-1/$3.50 |
| ☐ | #86: THE MYSTERY OF THE SILVER STAR | 64374-6/$3.50 |
| ☐ | #87: PROGRAM FOR DESTRUCTION | 64895-0/$3.99 |
| ☐ | #88: TRICKY BUSINESS | 64973-6/$3.99 |
| ☐ | #90: DANGER ON THE DIAMOND | 63425-9/$3.99 |
| ☐ | #91: SHIELD OF FEAR | 66308-9/$3.99 |
| ☐ | #92: THE SHADOW KILLERS | 66309-7/$3.99 |
| ☐ | #93: SERPENT'S TOOTH MYSTERY | 66310-0/$3.99 |
| ☐ | #95: DANGER ON THE AIR | 66305-4/$3.50 |
| ☐ | #97: CAST OF CRIMINALS | 66307-0/$3.50 |
| ☐ | #98: SPARK OF SUSPICION | 66304-6/$3.99 |
| ☐ | #101: MONEY HUNT | 69451-0/$3.99 |
| ☐ | #102: TERMINAL SHOCK | 69288-7/$3.99 |
| ☐ | #103: THE MILLION-DOLLAR NIGHTMARE | 69272-0/$3.99 |
| ☐ | #104: TRICKS OF THE TRADE | 69273-9/$3.99 |
| ☐ | #105: THE SMOKE SCREEN MYSTERY | 69274-7/$3.99 |
| ☐ | #106: ATTACK OF THE VIDEO VILLIANS | 69275-5/$3.99 |
| ☐ | #107: PANIC ON GULL ISLAND | 69276-3/$3.99 |
| ☐ | #110: THE SECRET OF SIGMA SEVEN | 72717-6/$3.99 |
| ☐ | #112: THE DEMOLITION MISSION | 73058-4/$3.99 |
| ☐ | #113: RADICAL MOVES | 73060-6/$3.99 |
| ☐ | #114: THE CASE OF THE COUNTERFEIT CRIMINALS | 73061-4/$3.99 |
| ☐ | #115: SABOTAGE AT SPORTS CITY | 73062-2/$3.99 |
| ☐ | #116:ROCK 'N' ROLL RENEGADES | 73063-0/$3.99 |
| ☐ | #117: THE BASEBALL CARD CONSPIRACY | 73064-9/$3.99 |
| ☐ | #118: DANGER IN THE FOURTH DIMENSION | 79308-X/$3.99 |
| ☐ | #119: TROUBLE AT COYOTE CANYON | 79309-8/$3.99 |
| ☐ | #120: CASE OF THE COSMIC KIDNAPPING | 79310-1/$3.99 |
| ☐ | #121: MYSTERY IN THE OLD MINE | 79311-X/$3.99 |
| ☐ | #122: CARNIVAL OF CRIME | 79312-8/$3.99 |
| ☐ | #123: ROBOT'S REVENGE | 79313-6/$3.99 |
| ☐ | #124: MYSTERY WITH A DANGEROUS BEAT | 79314-4/$3.99 |
| ☐ | #125: MYSTERY ON MAKATUNK ISLAND | 79315-2/$3.99 |
| ☐ | #126: RACING TO DISASTER | 87210-9/$3.99 |
| ☐ | #127: REEL THRILLS | 87211-7/$3.99 |
| ☐ | #128: DAY OF THE DINOSAUR | 87212-5/$3.99 |
| ☐ | #129: THE TREASURE AT DOLPHIN BAY | 87213-3/$3.99 |
| ☐ | #130: SIDETRACKED TO DANGER | 87214-1/$3.99 |
| ☐ | #132: MAXIMUM CHALLENGE | 87216-8/$3.99 |
| ☐ | #133: CRIME IN THE KENNEL | 87217-6/$3.99 |
| ☐ | #134: CROSS-COUNTRY CRIME | 50517-3/$3.99 |
| ☐ | #135: THE HYPERSONIC SECRET | 50518-1/$3.99 |
| ☐ | #136: THE COLD CASH CAPER | 50520-3/$3.99 |
| ☐ | #137: HIGH-SPEED SHOWDOWN | 50521-1/$3.99 |
| ☐ | #138: THE ALASKAN ADVENTURE | 50524-6/$3.99 |
| ☐ | #139: THE SEARCH FOR THE SNOW LEOPARD | 50525-4/$3.99 |
| ☐ | #140: SLAM DUNK SABOTAGE | 50526-2/$3.99 |
| ☐ | #141: THE DESERT THIEVES | 50527-0/$3.99 |
| ☐ | #142: LOST IN GATOR SWAMP | 00054-3/$3.99 |
| ☐ | #143: THE GIANT RAT OF SUMATRA | 00055-1/$3.99 |
| ☐ | #144: THE SECRET OF SKELETON REEF | 00056-X/$3.99 |
| ☐ | #145: TERROR AT HIGH TIDE | 00057-8/$3.99 |
| ☐ | THE HARDY BOYS GHOST STORIES | 69133-3/$3.99 |
| ☐ | #146: THE MARK OF THE BLUE TATTOO | 00058-6/$3.99 |
| ☐ | #147: TRIAL AND TERROR | 00059-4/$3.99 |
| ☐ | #148: THE ICE-COLD CASE | 00122-1/$3.99 |
| ☐ | #149: THE CHASE FOR THE MYSTERY TWISTER | 00123-X/$3.99 |

**LOOK FOR AN EXCITING NEW HARDY BOYS MYSTERY COMING FROM MINSTREL® BOOKS**

**Simon & Schuster, Mail Order Dept. HB5, 200 Old Tappan Rd., Old Tappan, N.J. 07675**

Please send me copies of the books checked. Please add appropriate local sales tax.

☐ Enclosed full amount per copy with this coupon (Send check or money order only)

☐ If order is $10.00 or more, you may charge to one of the following accounts: ☐ Mastercard ☐ Visa

Please be sure to include proper postage and handling: 0.95 for first copy; 0.50 for each additional copy ordered.

Name ____________________

Address ____________________

City ____________________ State/Zip ____________

Books listed are also available at your bookstore. Prices are subject to change without notice. 657-30